The CULLEN books by Mark Farrer (in chronological order):

Dirty Barry

Where Seagulls Dare

Bronchial Billy

A Fistful Of Collars

Pale Ale Rider

The Good The Bad & The Rugby

THE SHED POOL

mark farrer

funny business press

THE SHED POOL

ISBN: 978-1-9164892-8-8

Published by Funny Business Press

To the Professor and his team
For giving me the worst, and best, birthday ever.

This is a work of fiction.
Names, characters, places and incidents either are products of the author's imagination or are used fictitiously.
Any resemblance to actual events or locales or persons, living or dead, is entirely coincidental.
Except for Big Paul.

CONTENTS

ONE

"There's water in the shower!"

The frosted-glass bathroom door was an unwanted leftover from a recent double-glazing job, but it had fitted perfectly into the hole that had been there, once Paul had inserted a narrow shim of blazing orange "honeyed" pine he had similarly acquired. Shirley's voice boomed effortlessly through it.

"Glad to hear it." Paul beamed back. He had been under pain of death for longer than he could remember to get the plumbing sorted and a "working" shower working. Months had gone by. Apparently.

"No! Rainwater." Shirley appeared, a tangled damp mess in a heavy cream towel. All things considered she had unfortunately managed, with such scanty material, to cover all the main points. "Brown rainwater. In the tray."

"Oh." Paul looked up at this vision of annoyed and dishevelled loveliness and thought he had never seen anything so sexy in his entire life. Statuesque and shimmering, droplets clinging to her freckled shoulders, there was a shapeliness to her which outweighed her height and build. However, standing and approaching Shirley with what must have been more than a trace of lust on his face, she made it clear in no uncertain terms from her own expression that now was, most definitely, NOT the time. Paul's crest fell.

"I'll see what the problem is."

"Yes, lover. Do that." Shirley slumped against the doorframe and put her hands in her lap. "I can't keep doing this, you know?"

Paul, now elbow-deep in the trap under the shower, couldn't quite make out what she was saying: the tiling he had so meticulously laid from a surplus assortment of odd jobs may have covered the walls and floor completely but the acoustics of the room were now somewhat superior to being sat at the very back of Liverpool Anglican cathedral and trying to catch the sermon from the Catholic one. Slightly. "Sorry, babe - what?"

Shirley's bedraggled locks appeared in his peripheral vision. "I said - what're you doing down there?"

Paul looked up at her, eyebrows raised, his face inches from the shower tray. "Looking to see where the water's coming in from."

"Huh." Shirley sniffed, unimpressed. "Call me a layman but I always thought that water acted under gravity and thus moved from higher to lower." She jerked her head upwards to the ceiling tiles, acquired as part of a second's lot off the back of a friend's lorry - a Travis Perkins delivery that had not been missed. For several days, anyway.

"Yes, babe. But I thought perhaps there was some waste water upwelling or summat - the water being brown an' that?"

"You saying I'm trying to have a shower in shit!" Shirley was appalled and fought back a gag reflex.

"No, no, no." Paul lied quickly. "Groundwater seeping back up the pipes... due to... pressure differences and... perhaps a blockage." He forced a smile. "It's all good natural water here, my love. Straight from the Glentress hills, pure and Scottish. Nothing nasty."

"No, sweetheart. I can't do this anymore." Shirley looked sincerely upset but genuinely determined.

"What?"

"Live like this." She gestured around, vaguely, at everything.

"Like what?" Paul was genuinely puzzled as he gave his personally-constructed palace a brief once-over. Constructed from cast-offs and bits and pieces he had acquired from, ahem, various sources, it was more than just a wooden single-storey with mismatched windows and the odd bit of plastic sheeting still protruding from sundry corners. It was, a remarkable physical embodiment of the man himself. Like a beaver building a dam, or a bower bird a nest, he had managed to create something which summed him up and presented his personality to the world. A phantasmagorical contrivance showing skill, creativity, resourcefulness and desire for a partner. You could almost call it modern art. Certainly, like a Picasso, not everything in Paul's cabin was exactly where it was supposed to be. Some might call it shonky or unfinished but it was Paul's pride and joy. Nestled amongst its neighbours on the slopes above Soonhope Burn, he had built handrailed steps down the valley sides to approach it and a substantial deck area at the rear from which to barbecue and drink beer when the setting sun decided to appear and bathe the property in warmth. He'd even tapped into water and electricity supplies which fed his neighbours so that all modern conveniences could be catered for. The fact that Scottish Borders Council knew nothing about it, or him, was just the icing on this particular cake.

As a result it was almost impossible for Paul not to see his cabin as a wonderful, perfect edifice. Like someone with advancing cataracts, the more he had done running repairs - snagging, is all it was really - the more he saw only the small detail, the effort and love he had put into it. The overall picture was blurred and lost.

"Lover." She pulled him to her, sinking to her haunches as she did so. She was about to pat his hand when she realised where it had just been. "Paul. This... isn't me! It's lovely and sweet and all. And all you! I can see that. Every nail you've hammered, every plank you've planed, every bead of sweat you've wiped from your brow. But it's just not..."

"What?"

"Finished!"

"It's getting there though, babe." Paul face was swiftly eaten once more by his enormous smile.

"I know, Paul. I know." She took his huge face in her hands, trying to match his smile but just shaking her head sadly. "It is. But are we?"

Paul frowned and looked away from her, perhaps trying to find the gist of what she was saying in the beams of light filtering in through the frosted window. "I don't..."

"Lover." Shirley said, her voice quiet and still.

"Um?" Paul stared into her face, the light fast-fading from his usually gleaming eyes. Shirley pursed her lips and tilted her head downwards, as if looking at him over invisible reading glasses. This was a sign Paul recognised, a sign becoming increasingly familiar. Shirley was taking charge, about to lead him down a conversation stairwell, one she had led him down before, where she was the adult and he was some kind of lumbering circus bear. Taking him by the hand and guiding him slowly down because he wasn't able to grasp the handrail of their conversation and was too intellectually weak to be trusted to manage the steps on his own. And he was too big for a stair gate.

"Which is going to be finished first? This house or us?"

Instinctively, Paul slipped into his role. "This house?"

"Good answer."

Paul blew out his cheeks with relief.

"And when do you suppose that will be?" Shirley prodded.

"Soon?"

Shirley locked onto his eyes and shook her head ever-so-slightly. "Do you know how soon?"

"Um."

"Let me tell you."

Here it came. A kind of invisible authority she could switch on at will. He had watched her do this and wondered where it came from and what it was. Maybe it was from being surrounded by insufferably tasty pastry everyday - you had to develop a steel will or succumb when you worked at Greggs. God knows Paul wouldn't have been able to show the self-restraint his lover did in her position. You could see it in her face, her frame, her stance. Hear it in her voice. She radiated it, even when she wasn't looking at you. It was something utterly mysterious to him and, more than once recently, when he had had trouble sleeping, he had looked over at her slumbering form and marvelled at her. She didn't radiate this power when she was asleep, obviously, but it was still there. Detectable and tangible yet tantalisingly out of reach to him. It was like sleeping next to an Infinity Stone.

"It will be finished before I set foot in this place again." Shirley instructed.

"Um."

"Paul?"

Paul found himself slowly nodding. "Yes."

"If you want to be with me, see me after work or whatever, you will have to come to mine. Is that clear?"

Shirley didn't wait for an answer. She rose up to her full height, leaving Paul down near the shower tray staring into space, and padded out, dripping, back into the living room.

Keith sighed heavily and looked exaggeratedly at his watch. Bryan Metcalfe glanced up from the agenda and notepad in front of him and glared.

"Somewhere to be, Keith?" Bryan snipped. "Don't want to keep you." His voice was dry, high-pitched, almost whiny - like listening to an old gramophone record played on a cheese grater.

Keith was in his early fifties - quite the whippersnapper amongst the Walkerburn Allotment crowd. Most were retired, Bryan himself was in his seventies, many still lived in the houses they had grown up in, married Walkerburn lasses, and never *ever* thought of leaving. Keith had never, ever thought of leaving the town and had been the proudest father when his daughter, Poppy, was the Walkerburn Lass - an annual appointment bestowed on a primary schoolgirl who represented all that was fair and good about the town and whose ceremonial duties for the year consisted of posing in ludicrous costumes for photos while opening fetes and the like. And it had been Bryan himself, as a newly-elected Councillor, who had announced Poppy's appointment and bestowed the sash on her.

"Can we just wrap this up, Bryan? It's been bloody hours. All this procedure and bureaucracy. Bloody points of order?"

"We need to do this properly. We are a committee. With funds. A constitution. Written minutes and an obligation to declare-"

"I'd like to bloody declare!" Keith wagged an outraged digit towards the Chair. "Declare I'm sick of all this palaver. Let's just get on, get done and get down the pub or get off home."

Even from where he was sitting, several yards away, from the comfort and safety of the committee table up on the stage, Bryan could see the dirt under and around Keith's fingernails. Allotment dirt. A loamy soil, fertile and well-suited to runner beans, radishes, carrots and whatever else Keith, Bryan and the other allotment owners cared to nurture.

Bryan had no truck with dirt and slovenliness. He had spent thirty-five years in industry, tidily turned out every day: herringbone jacket, grey Farah trousers, a heavy woollen tie at the neck of a checked shirt tucked into a lambswool cardigan. It amounted to a uniform for him, one that had come to define him and his occupation - they were one and the same in his day. You went to a party, got interviewed on TV, appeared on a game show: what was the first question anyone asked you after your name? What do you do? He was what he was and he dressed for that role, in and out of the office. Neatness and punctuality, precision and attention to detail - that was how you got the job done, whether it was running a Quality Management team or chairing the Walkerburn Allotment Group - you most definitely did not get the job done by rocking up and spouting the odds with dirt under your fingernails. You could tell the fibre of a man by the shine on his shoes and Keith's scuffed work-boots were hardly inspiring.

Bryan pulled the glasses down his nose, their security ensured by the attached safety chain he wore around his neck, and peered at this irritant, a regular irritant, always sat in the front row. Sometimes it was tuts, sometimes it was sucking loudly on sweets, sometimes exasperated sighing which resonated around the spartan village hall with no soft furnishings of any kind to deaden the sound. Just wood-laminate flooring and oak cross-beams to support the roof, rows of contoured red plastic chairs which screeched when you moved them, and a tea-trolley in the corner carrying cold white IKEA cups and saucers, and a large stainless-steel urn. The only non-rigid materials in the place were the clothes each of the committee were wearing and the small wicker basket on the trolley containing tiny cartons of UHT milk.

"If I may be permitted to speak for the rest of the committee-" Bryan began.

"It's getting bloody dark!"

"These are not simple matters to tick off without due-"

"Of course they're bloody simple! There's a waiting list for allotments, and when an allotment comes up for grabs it gets allocated to the next person on the list! What's complicated about that?"

"My pal Frankie's on a council-run allotment down in Peebles." Geoff, emboldened by Keith's interjections next to him, nodded nervously. "He says they never have any of this malarkey. It's all done reg'lar."

"Aye. The sooner we get our scheme enrolled with the council the better." Keith affirmed, folding his arms.

"Which, as we all know, is itself complicated by the fact that-"

"Bloody complications! Bugger off with your

complications, man." Keith uncrossed his arms and stood, gesturing around to the sparsely attended seats behind him. "We don't need complications, do we? We need bloody action! All those in favour-"

"Mr Knox!" Bryan stood and slammed his pen down on the table. "We have procedures here, and an agenda of items to adhere to. There will be no spontaneous voting on any issue which, as Veronica will attest, cannot anyway be undertaken without first tabling such a motion at least three days prior to any meeting." Bryan didn't bother looking around at Veronica as he knew she would be nodding in agreement. He knew the rules inside-out, largely because he had made most of them himself. "If we can just get back to item number 12 we can, as you request, get this wrapped up and off home before it gets dark."

"Feckin' unbelievable." Keith shook his head wearily. "Albert's well shut of all this, I can tell you. God Rest His Soul."

Bryan glared at him. "I see no reason to bring up-"

"No reason! This is what pushed him over the edge, probably. All this!" Keith threw his sheaf of papers up into the air and they fluttered down around him as he continued to shout. "Months he'd waited for a buggering allotment. Bloody months! And he could've had one straight away if it hadn't been for all this bollocking stuff. But it's all too late now, isn't it? He's in the feckin' ground with the cabbages and turnips. Closest to an allotment he ever got."

Keith sat down and shuffled in his seat, muttering, defeated.

Bryan took a deep breath. It was sad about Albert right enough but Bryan resented the implication - the ludicrous implication - that his due process might in any way have contributed to Albert's eventual demise through natural causes. He'd been a kindly old gent but hardly the type who'd have made much out of an allotment at his age. Much better that the allotment be useful to Bryan instead - which it had been and would continue to be as long as he could keep order and maintain due process. It was called due process - and Bryan never lost enthusiasm when explaining this to anyone - because process was due.

"If we can try and keep interruptions to a minimum?" Bryan suggested, scanning the hall. "Andy? I believe you have the financial statement for the month to summarise?"

"What are you up to today then, lover?"

Shirley was bending over at the waist, towelling her hair like she was belt-sanding a skirting board. She had a whole separate towel reserved for her copious hair, thick as it was - her hair, not the towel. So copious was it, in fact, that she could afford to leave strands of it on every surface in her flat - and Paul's cabin also when she stayed over. Paul gave a rueful pout as he mentally adjusted the tense of that thought: when she *had* stayed over. No further conversation on the subject had occurred on this subject and Paul wasn't in a hurry to raise it again. She had taken all her things back to her flat, he had gathered up a few of his and now he was lodging with her more or less full-time. At least until he had repaired his roof. He steered himself away from this sad corner of his brain and watched Shirley again.

Paul marvelled at this female chore, not one he had had to personally bother himself with since... oh, well, he couldn't remember when he'd last had what you could call long hair. His chiselled and smoothly trimmed dome,

Number Two all over, was like moleskin. He may have a high forehead but male pattern baldness had yet to come calling and his hair was scalp-tidy and perfect. Never ruffled, never scruffy, just shiny, sleek and velvety black. Paul never had anything even approaching bedhead or a bad hair day - hadn't even been aware of these terms as actual things in the world until Shirley had educated him in the ways of the follicularly well-endowed. He was able to spring out of bed, or stagger depending on his situation, look in the mirror and see himself as he always was. That was his superpower and he wondered musingly whether Shirley might be jealous of it. His gaze drifted back to her now as she lifted her head to look enquiringly at him. He realised she must have asked him a question.

"Hmm?"

"Today? What are you going to do?"

"Ah, well." Paul contemplated the ceiling as if it held some detailed notes he'd left there the night before - amazingly brilliant, thought-provoking notes which could somehow describe a useful arc to get him from his current state of working-man-with-no-working-vehicle to gainfully-employed-earner-with-busy-day-ahead-of-him. Alas, someone had removed the notes in the night. "No van you see."

"Yes, I know." Shirley gave a tight smile at her beloved. "Hence my question."

"Right. Well, I'll have to slope back home - take the dogs for a walk, obv."

"Obv." Shirley's smiled relaxed, her eyes twinkling at Paul's fondness for his Jack Russells, Ant and Dec.

"Check for any mail an' that."

"And?"

"Er... well, I guess I could come back here and see how

Keith's getting on with the van. He didn't actually tell me how long it was going to take."

"Did he say how much it was going to cost?"

"Erm, not exactly no. He said he needed to check it out first." Paul blagged. "But it'll be mate's rates, for sure."

Shirley sighed as she reached for her hairbrush. "Not going to be working on your cabin then?"

In a belated flash Paul remembered the roof leak he was supposed to be repairing. "Oh aye! That? Goes without saying doesn't it? Implied. Got to do that."

Shirley's mouth widened into another smile, but her eyes seemed strangely unamused. She stood watching him for a moment, but when he resolutely stayed put she shook her head almost invisibly, the slightest frown skittering across her face and then disappearing. "Super. Oh Christ - look at the time!" Shirley hurriedly fastened a blouse while squeezing her feet into a pair of trainers. "Going to miss my bus. See you later, lover."

She leant over and kissed his forehead and Paul caught a distractingly fulsome glimpse of cleavage before she whisked herself away in an engulfing cloud of Semichem's finest Eau de Toilette.

Paul waited until he heard the front door close and then gave a deep breath, flinging back the duvet to reveal dark, muscled legs covered in black hair. He swung his feet over the side of the bed, a sudden determination for the day tearing into him, only to grimace as his left foot touched the floor and a slice of pain shot through him. Gingerly he eased himself up into a standing position and tottered to the bathroom.

He sat on the porcelain, glad to have the weight off his foot, and pondered his first move. That initial determination was now tempered by reality. Getting all the way back to his cabin on foot was not going to be on today's agenda. If he was going to tend to his beloved dogs he needed transport so: first step, see what Keith had to say about his van.

"Technical term for it? Buggered." Keith didn't believe in breaking news gently. It wasn't his way. He may have looked almost cherubic - his currant-bun eyes, round and intelligent, usually shone from his face with either annoyance or frustration, but seldom restraint. His short grey hair, razored to a medium-length stubble had a prominent clump on the top of his head which refused to take anything lying down - much like Keith himself - and always seemed to have something to say for itself. The result was that Keith looked a bit like an aged Oor Wullie - slightly jowly, red cheeks from constant exposure to the cold (whether it be the chill of his workplace or the outdoors of the allotment), and permanently attired in old overalls.

"Oh." Paul was crestfallen. "Thanks, mate."

"Look, Beep. It's not like I've buggered it meself. It's just old." Paul was known to many as Big Paul - standing 6'5" with the heft of a beefy Highlander will get you such a moniker. His friends shortened this to BP and his close friends shortened this further to Beep. Keith had known Paul since High School.

"So'm I."

"Aye, well. Not of us are getting any younger, am I right?"

Paul felt a twinge in his left foot as if in evidence of that very fact and he winced. Keith took this as a sign of agreement and ploughed on. "It's been cutting out, then it runs fine, then it cuts out?"

"Yep."

"Well, looks to me like fuel contamination."

"You saying I put the wrong fuel in?"

"No, I'm saying you've got water leaking into the fuel system. Contaminating it."

"Oh, right."

"And, by the looks of it, it's been happening a while, yeah?"

"Six months?" Paul sucked his teeth, thinking *more like a year.*

"Well that, my friend, is going to cost you."

"Huh?"

"Look. Problem like this..." Keith wiped his hands on a tea-towel and picked up a cold mug of tea. "Sooner it gets dealt with the better. You leave it too long - like it looks like you have - and the repair cost is higher."

"How much... higher?" Paul swallowed.

"Well, if you'd brought it in earlier, probably could've just done a system flush. Couple of hundred maybe. Now though..."

"Couple of hundred?"

"But now. Well, you're gonna need new injectors, new pump. Maybe new pipes as well.

Paul felt his forehead moisten and he blew out his cheeks. "How much?" He said in a low voice.

"Fifteen hundred."

"Fifteen-!" Paul was gasping for air. "That's more than the bleedin' van's worth!"

"Might be able to get it down to twelve. And if the pipes don't need doing..."

"Twelve hundred quid! Still more than it's worth." Paul wanted to cry.

"If you took it to a dealer they'd charge you double that."

"Yeah, well I'm as likely to take it to a dealer as I am to find twelve hundred quid."

"Like I said, Beep. If you'd brought it in earlier..." Keith gave a sad smile and large shrug of his shoulders. He was a mechanic by trade, and a bloody good one. Cheap, reliable and flexible. Most folk in Walkerburn and the adjoining towns had used his services for years and had no intention of changing. His garage was one of a number of rundown buildings on a small industrial estate which had sprung up on the site of the old mill. Draughty, echoing and in need of repair - and that was just Keith.

"I need the van for work. If I don't have the van, I don't work. If I don't work I don't have twelve hundred quid." Paul shook his head, gazing absently at the oil-stained floor of the workshop. Then he looked up at Keith. "Do you know how long it takes me to earn that much?"

"Tell me about it, mate." Keith grimaced. "And even when I earn it I have to spend it on heating this place." He stretched his arms out and appealed to the heavens or, at least, the cobwebbed and rusting eaves which supported the manky corrugated-iron roof panels.

Paul surveyed Keith's garage and sighed in empathy. "Aye. Bills innit? Life is nothing but bills."

"Bills is right. Mind, it's all bloody bollocks this leccy bill o' mine." Keith spat onto the floor and wiped his mouth with the back of a dirty hand.

Paul looked around the freezing space, two disconsolate cars up on examination platforms and a rickety table over by the sliding doors with a kettle coming to the boil. "Aye, heating isn't cheap. Inflation an' that."

"Bollocks to inflation. I know I need to have electric

heaters all over the place and that's not the most efficient way of staying warm."

"It ain't warm in here!"

"No, I fecking know it's not. Can't afford to have them on more than a bit each day."

"Aye."

"Aye an' then some." Keith said. "But the fecker's gone through the bloody roof this last six months. Doubled since last year! That's not fecking inflation - that's thieving bollocks!"

"Doubled?"

"Aye. Doubled. I've complained and asked them to double-check and that but they don't even come out and look. Just go through the readings and say, no it's all above board. Above board my arse."

They both wandered over to the table and Keith made two fresh mugs of tea. In the cold autumn air outside the half-open garage door, Paul could see a few hardy souls digging and scratching in the allotments beyond the metal railings, ferrying wheelbarrows to and fro. A watery sun cast pale shadows and the air was ripe with the smell of strong compost.

"What would you say if I could get your leccy bill down?" Paul asked.

"I'd say cheers mate. Much obliged."

"Would you say: And have this van repair on me?" Paul raised an eyebrow and waited for Keith's response.

"I'd say: don't talk bollocks, man! Wipe out £1200 for getting me bills down a bit?"

"Wiping out £1200 for getting your bills down *a lot*." Paul corrected, bending in closer and lowering his voice. "Maybe getting them down to zero."

Keith frowned but let his eyes swivel left and right

while his mind swam with possibilities. "How'd you do that then?"

"I'll show you." Paul's eyes gleamed and then he remembered himself. "Tomorrow. Got to go feed my dogs."

The rain smacked wetly against the window, condensation streaming down the inside, as Shirley sat ruminating at the back of the bus. From her usual seat over the wheel arch she stared vacantly out at the grey smear of open countryside on the short journey to Peebles. Something was definitely up; she could smell it.

Her nose was especially keen, well-trained as it was from hours spent sniffing lairy schoolkids crowding her small branch of Greggs each lunchtime, hovering near the door in thickets of intrigue, all seemingly intent on nicking baguettes and bottles of peach Oasis from the chiller cabinet. Okay, so she had done the same when she was a kid, and it wasn't so much the smell of suspicion but the look - the air of overdone insouciance, unnecessarily loud conversation or laughter, snatched glances to left and right when no-one thought she was looking. That tingling sensation she got when there was shenanigans afoot, was one she never failed to recognise - ears pricked, mentally up on the balls of her feet. And she felt it now, not from the thoughts of nervous miscreants in school uniform, but from this morning's behaviour of her lover and partner. And other mornings. What was this reluctance to get out of bed until she had left for work? She felt sure he was hiding something, but what?

As the bus swayed and rattled along beside the turgid Tweed, she brought to mind a whole host of other little signs and signals she had been picking up and nursing for a while now. Ever since they had come back from the Dominican Republic actually. When was that, six months ago was it? Here a shifty glance, there an odd pause - like he was self-editing his sentences before speaking them aloud. Then there was the overdone bright-and-breeziness that, while it was Paul's stock in trade, was now somehow just... off. Only by a little, but definitely off.

It was this unease, as much as anything, which had perhaps triggered her exasperated comments to him back in his cabin a few weeks ago: dishing out her ultimatum and hot-footing it back to her own little flat, leaving him puffing and gasping in her wake if he wanted to stay over.

Which, of course, he did.

She didn't miss Paul's cabin, truth be told, and clearing some space in her own bedroom to allow Paul to leave clothes and toiletries at hers was no obstacle. She had been genuine about not wanting to live in a semi-permanent state of incompleteness, although she had surprised herself with her declaration that their relationship was going nowhere. But there it was, and the minute she had uttered it she realised it was truly how she felt and it made her sad and slightly tearful to think that their relationship might just sputter out, grind slowly to a stop - like his bloody van. Paul was like her phone: since she'd had it, they had both slowed down, stopped working unexpectedly, and now seemed no longer able to reliably complete simple tasks.

But such was the man - her man - and she did love him.

But look at his lack of drive and ambition - just look at the state his van was in and how he drags his feet over repairing his cabin. Maybe her mother was right? Ah, but which contradictory yet strongly held (not to mention expressed) view of her mother's was it? That was her mother's stock-in-trade: holding mutually exclusive opinions which she hurled violently around, inflicting pain and shame on her daughter like someone not entirely in control of their paintball automatic.

See, on the one hand Paul was just not good enough for her daughter. No-one could be. This Paul of hers was an idler, a slacker, a slob with all the appeal of the month-old bottom of a fridge salad drawer - who probably smelled little better. On the other hand, Shirley was a forty-something single woman with a big build (one of her mother's favourite phrases, brandished with an air of astonishment since neither of Shirley's parents had been large themselves - wherever did she get it from?) This Paul was resourceful, faithful and decent. What was she waiting for: Brad Pitt to realise he had been fishing in the wrong sea and wade over to pluck her from the Tweed like some kind of marvellous find?

This constant flip-flop of viewpoints which she heard endlessly from her mother - *dead-in-a-ditch* Paul versus *don't-miss-out* Paul - made Shirley's headspin. God knows what her mother was going to conclude if she actually got around to *meeting* him! And which of these two Pauls was up to something? Because sure as eggs were eggs he was up to something. Something was amiss and she was going to get to the bottom of it. Decent and kind-hearted he might be but, perhaps as a result, he was a bloody awful liar.

Casting back once more to their recent Dominican Republic trip (the memory marred somewhat by the unfortunate incident with some sniffer dogs at the airport) she could swear she had spotted a small box making its way from his suitcase to his sock drawer, but later when she had gone to sneak a look while Paul was in the pool, it had not been there. What had she hoped to find? An engagement ring, of course! And how would that make her feel - about Paul, about their relationship? Shirley was immediately struck by how clearly this single thought, this simple hypothesis, sliced through her doubts and made her confusion vanish. There was her answer, staring her in the face: she'd be delighted, thrilled, touched and fulfilled. And, in addition, she would feel finally *loved.* That would put paid to the mewling flip-floppery of comments from her mother, oh yes. An engagement ring would be a truly marvellous thing to find.

Shirley closed her eyes and tried to recall what she'd seen. Or what she hoped she'd seen. Like a small child in bed on Christmas Eve, she screwed her eyes up tightly and wished and wished. Not for Santa, but for the scene in her head to play out again and show her a clear image. She let the swaying of the bus soothe her as she mentally compiled a list of possible hiding places she could search when she got home from work. In her mind's eye, she saw herself slide open a drawer to find a small, precious container nestling amongst the socks.

TWO

Under a grey sky struggling to fend off the dawn, Bryan got to work. It was too risky doing this in the dark. Not because it was hard to see what you were doing - playing around with high voltage electricity wasn't something you undertook lightly even in perfect visibility - but because his portable light enabling him to work could be seen by others, and because of the noise he might make at this early hour. The safest time to do this was early morning - at 5am there were few folk about and plenty of reasons why a sudden noise, loud clatter or suchlike wouldn't wake people deep into their REM sleep, and plenty of alibis (foxes, cats, etc) if they did.

He smiled to himself as he pulled the wrench from his trusty toolbelt and set to work. It was always a trip down memory lane this bit, sweeping him back to the earliest days of his public sector career. His training as an apprentice with Southern Scotland Electricity Board had shown him how to manipulate supplies safely, so that taps and extensions could be put in place, routing electricity down a new line. He'd been somewhat rusty, given the years that had passed since then, so on his first tap he had been nervous and sweaty - not convinced he had done it right until he was delighted to find it had worked. But from then on Bryan had just got faster and smoother - these taps weren't invisible but they would pass scrutiny by any member of the public, or a bog-standard meter reader come to that. Anyone with an expert eye *who was looking for them* would take one look at his handiwork, neat and tidy though it may be, and recognise it for what it was: an illegal, surrogate tap which diverted power from an existing supply.

He smiled as he worked but his smile faded as he reflected on the bitter end to this same career. He had long ago progressed from humble apprentice, up and along a contorted trajectory until he had secured a middle-management position from where he had planned to retire on a full pension - only to be made redundant a few years short of his actual retirement date. He winced and spat at the recollection of his treatment at the hands of those bastards! All the more reason to be pleased with the fact that he was stealing from them now and they would never know. The SSEB may have been reorganised and rebranded as Scottish Power but is was the very same bastards he had no doubt. Revenge was, indeed, a dish best served cold.

He finished the tap, swept up the debris and offcut cable strips into his bag, and whistled gently as he strolled out into the very early light.

"Babe?" Paul said. "Do you trust me?"

"Of course, lover." Shirley didn't look up while she rifled behind the cushions and down the back of her sofa.

"You sure?"

"Lumpa." Shirley stopped her search, stood up, smiled and hustled towards him, extending an enormous hug. She only called him an oompa-lumpa when she was genuinely expressing heartfelt affection. They shared a mighty embrace - two fleshy oil tankers wrapped snugly, mere millimeters to spare, inside the Panama canal of her cosy flat.

"It's just..." He mumbled through her thick hair now blanketing his chest.

"Hmm?"

"Well, you know..."

"No lover, I don't." Shirley pulled slightly away so she could look up into his face. Even for someone of her stature - 5'10" was tall for a woman, God knows she'd found that out in her many attempts to secure a partner - it still required craning her neck sometimes in order to catch the eyes gleaming up there at Paul's towering height. She thought they made a grand couple - a Venti couple in fact. She was broad and heavyset, but shapely with it: she knew that she had curves, perhaps too many, but they were in proportion to the rest of her and she knew she definitely *scrubbed up well,* as they said. She wasn't a classical beauty but she certainly wasn't plain - her eyes were her best feature, she felt: bright, green and twinkly. While her nose was her worst - too large she thought and rather hooked, giving her profile a little too much of the look of Punch. Or perhaps Judy.

But Paul - God bless him - thought she was beautiful as she was. At least, she thought he did. He never actually used the word *beautiful*, preferring *smashing* or *grand.* She sighed, accepting. "What's up?"

Paul stood somewhat stiffly while she engulfed him. "Nothing."

"Cool." She said, and whisked away through to the bedroom to check again on that pesky sock drawer.

"Been looking for you!" Big Paul plonked himself down next to Cullen on the bench overlooking the Tweed where it boiled and writhed down a small weir into a stone-filled pool. He stretched out his left leg and gingerly waggled his foot. "Bleeding foot's killing me."

"Huh."

"Went to your caravan and everything."

"Fancy."

"Yeah." Paul's dogs, Ant and Dec, sniffed around the bench, then Cullen's feet. He was wearing his standard issue lime-green Berghaus waterproof, torn and worn in places and long past its best, beneath his battered leather cowboy hat. His old brown walking boots had similarly seen better days and Paul wondered what scent his pets could detect by such close proximity to them. The thought bothered him, but not his dogs, who - satisfied that Cullen was not an enemy, a threat or a source of food - mooched off into more interesting undergrowth. Paul watched them go and then suddenly lit up. "Ooh, yeah: it's gone!"

"My caravan?"

"Yep. Checked. Not there."

"Not where?"

"Where it should be."

Cullen looked at Paul, weighing him up. "Where should it be?"

"Well, where it was. You know."

Cullen sighed. "Moved it."

"What?"

"I moved it."

"Why?"

"Because you keep looking for me."

"Funny. But, hey - that's great!"

"Unh. Well, you found me anyway, so..."

"No, I mean it's great that it's still in, er... movable condition."

"Of course it is."

"Listen. I've seen it, remember. It's only the stains that are keeping it together."

Cullen scowled. "I'm assuming you have a point here. Otherwise..."

"'Course. See, I need a great hiding place. And what better place than one that not only can't be found but, when you try to find it, it's gone! Perfect." Paul beamed his most energetic grin, eyes twinkling above his smartly-trimmed goatee, panther black.

Cullen squinted into the brilliance of his friend's vim and enthusiasm, the glare dazzling him.

"A hiding place?"

"Correctamundo."

"For what?" Paul could swear his friend's ears were pricked.

"A certain something."

"How certain?"

"Er, what?"

"How certain a something?"

"Mate, you might need to put some nouns or verbs in there. Not sure that sentence means anything. To me, anyway."

"When you say *a certain something* it conjures up images of something I'm not certain I want to entertain in my caravan."

"Entertain?"

"Indulge me."

"Ok. Well..." Paul shifted uneasily, looking at the ground, letting his voice drop. "It's a secret."

"A secret?"

"You know, personal like."

Cullen pursed his lips. "Would this personal secret be... herbal, at all?"

Paul bunched up his whiskery lips like a peeved sea-lion whose mackerel had been thrown into the next pen. "You never forget do you?"

Cullen shook his head. "Nor do I forgive."

"Helpful. Not." Cullen waited. "Look, that was years ago, ok?" Paul's huge hands weighed an invisible package in front of him.

"I know."

"Never to be repeated."

"I know." That sounded worryingly like a threat. Paul looked at his friend's face - the same creases and lines, weathered cheeks and steel-grey eyes piercing him. Was Cullen taking the piss, refusing his help or agreeing to his request? Paul had absolutely no fucking idea. There was no way to tell sometimes so Paul deferred to his natural optimism and his default strategy of grinning a lot. It didn't usually work with Shirley. Nor with his customers. In fact, now he came to think about it, he was struggling to recall when or if it had ever worked. Davy fell for it, perhaps? But imagination not being Paul's long suit, he wasn't going to waste valuable brain space trying to crack open another approach. This one would have to do.

"Cool." Paul smiled and exhaled loudly, a weight off his chest. "So where is it, then?"

"Where's what?"

"Your bloody caravan!"

Cullen stalled. "Why do you need to hide something in my caravan?"

Paul thrust his chin forward, exasperated. "Shirley's rooting through my stuff. Pockets, drawers, everything.

She's like a bleeding store detective."

"She does work at Greggs."

"So? I'm not one of her bloody employees." He sat back and threw his chest out. "I'm trustworthy."

"So why doesn't she trust you?"

"Huh." Paul considered this as if for the first time. "Good question that."

"And the answer is...?"

"Fecked if I know."

"Could it be because the words *never to be repeated* are often repeated?"

"Look, you gonna help me or not?"

"Why don't you hide this certain something in your van?"

"Can't. Van's in the shop. Big job."

"Right. How you going to pay for that then?"

Paul gave what he hoped was a mysterious look. "I have my way and means."

"Right." Cullen said, disbelievingly. "So you want to hide something - in my caravan - that you don't want Shirley to find?"

"Correct."

"A secret?"

"Correctamundo."

"Because if Shirley found it...?"

Paul sucked his teeth. "I don't want her to find it."

"Why not?"

"Because."

"Because...?"

"Just because, ok?"

Cullen's eyes narrowed. "Do you promise that your previous ill-judged decision to store stuff in my caravan-"

"Years ago" Paul interrupted.

"Years ago. Will never be repeated?"

"Yes."

"Tell me again about the sniffer dogs. At the airport."

Paul sulked. "That was a misunderstanding!"

"Hmm." The silence dragged. Paul looked at his friend's cold, calculating eyes, first the left, then the right, then back to the left.

"Well?"

The silence dragged. "No." Cullen said finally.

"What?"

"No."

"Really?"

"Really."

"Mate, are you seriously telling me that you won't let me store something in your caravan? Not even temporarily?"

"Correct."

Paul's face ran the gamut of emotions from A to A: aghast, astonished, appalled. "What - don't you trust me or something?"

"Correct." Cullen didn't blink. "Amundo."

"How do you know all this, then? 'Bout leccy." Keith asked the following morning. He scratched noisily at the unkempt hair on his jaw, loosening some grey flakes which settled on his navy overalls. It wasn't a beard yet but it matched his haircut, his whole stubbled head a mottled ball of fuzz.

"Let's just say I've had some experience in the matter."

"You've done it yourself, you mean?" Keith's brown eyes sparkled with a keen interest.

"Not exactly. Jimmy Two-Sheds, works down the

council?"

"Jimmy down the Bowls Club?"

"The very same. He showed me. Used to do it all the time apparently - back in the old days. Says it's still very popular in developing countries. India, an' that."

"Get away."

"Yup. No-one pays for power out there. S'why the place is a buzzin' melting pot of entrepreneurs." Paul recited, recalling Jimmy's exact words.

"Well, I'll be." Keith put down his mug of tea and wiped his hands on his overalls, making both dirtier in the process. His sleeves were rolled up to above the elbow revealing copious tattoos of somewhat inconsistent quality. Paul thought his arms looked like the pad Shirley kept beside the phone. "Well, come on then! Show us - time is money with this bloody leccy bill. Every second wasted is costing me dear."

Paul finished his tea and wiped the drips from his moustache on the back of a mighty hand. "Lead on then, our Keith. Show me where your meter is."

Keith led him outside and along the exterior of the building, a tight squeeze between the workshop wall and the tall metal fence that separated the industrial estate from the allotments. The grass here was overgrown with weeds and brambles, and it was tough going for these two big men to thrust their way through.

"Should get those allotment fellas to hack away some of this stuff." Paul grumbled to Keith's back.

"Hey! I'm one o' those allotment fellas."

"Oh aye? Green fingers is it?"

"Some days. When I'm not trying to earn the money to pay these feckin' bills. And when I'm not busting my arse tending one of the dormant plots."

"What's a dormant plot?"

"It's an allotment waiting to be allocated to a new owner. Mister Bryan-with-a-y feckin' Metcalfe has all us members tending the unused ones on some kind of caretaker system. Need to keep 'em from getting overgrown in case it puts people off wanting to acquire them."

"Not much demand then - no new members?" Paul toyed briefly with the idea of applying for a plot as something he and Shirley could share. Then an image of him pulling carrots and cauliflowers out of the cold soil into a wheelbarrow seared into his head and he immediately abandoned the fancy.

"Don't make me laugh. There's a waiting list a mile long. Getting one o' these is like winning the lottery."

"So why are there these dormant ones then?"

Keith paused for a moment and then looked at Paul angrily. "Because our fecker Metcalfe controls the allotments with an iron grip. He's got us all tangled up in rules and regs and points o' order and constitutional amendments and... oh, don't get me started. All you need to know is that there's a load of allotments lying idle and getting hold of one is like prying it from a dead man's hand - if only Metcalfe would do the decent thing and snuff it."

They reached a large grey cabinet attached to the outside wall. "There you are." Keith waved at the mildewed box as it if it were the main prize on a game show. "Mine's bottom right."

"Okey-dokey. Let's have a butcher's." Paul struggled to a squat, his overalls riding up as they dragged on the fence behind him.

"Ere, do you need to me give you a lift home? If you're leaving your van here."

"Nah, it's alright. Stopping at Shirl's." Paul nodded his head backwards, Shirley's flat being clearly visible in the row of terraces bordering one side of the allotment ground.

"Oh aye!" Keith leered. "Going well is it then? Moving in together. Cosy."

"Well..." Paul struggled to get a purchase on the cabinet door, feeling wedged in to an overtight space like a child stuck down a well. "It is going alright, aye. Not moving in as such, mind. My roof's leaking. She won't stay there with a leaky roof. Not..." He struggled for the exact word she had used. "Seemly."

"Ooh, seemly!" Keith clutched at imaginary pearls. "This is just Walkerburn. She does know that right? It's not fecking Morningside."

"She knows. She wants to better herself. Nowt wrong wi' that. Although she wants me to better meself too." He swung the cabinet door open with some difficulty and a little squealing of resistant rust. "That's got it."

"And here you are about to fiddle with my leccy supply." Keith stifled a laugh.

Paul glared at him. "Don't you dare say a word."

"Nah, you're alright Beep. Got to keep your woman happy, am I right?"

"Aye, well." Paul sighed, and then screwed his face up. "Ah."

"Oh aye." Keith put his hands on his hips, his dreams of money saved quickly evaporating. "Is that *Ah, I spoke too soon. Can't be done?* Or *Ah, it's going to be a bit trickier than I thought?*"

Paul stood up slowly, one knee making an audible crack, and pointed at the open cabinet. "It's *Ah, someone's beaten us to it.*"

"Not with you, mate?"

"The reason your electricity bills are so high, pal, is that someone has already tapped into yours!"

Councillor Bryan Metcalfe had no intention of getting angry; he was generally calmness and order personified. But this evening his normal studied equanimity was absent, his composure unsettled. He couldn't think calmly because his rheumatism was bothering him. The weather was damp and autumnal mists were settling in now that September was nearly over. That always made it worse, made his joints ache and freeze like he'd been given multiple novocaine injections that didn't work.

No, he had no time for anger. It was pointless, especially trying to use it to alleviate chronic rheumatic pain. What Bryan had time for - was, in fact, all about - were order and planning, structure, method and process. He had never met a procedure he didn't like and never found a task which didn't benefit from a checklist. Oh yes, if you wanted checklists, Bryan Metcalfe was the man for the job.

A working lifetime in quality control and management meant he would approach every task, any goal, with methodical practicality, calmness and efficiency. There was no point in getting annoyed or angry - that was just wasted energy and Bryan had no time *for* waste, and no time *to* waste. Through years of practice and application he had become the epitome of his cause. Like a toxin which infiltrated your nervous system: first the paperwork confused you - making you screw your face up and tilt your head trying to figure out just what paragraph 11.3b was trying to say with its references to ISO9001:2008 and its insistence on a counter-signature at the foot of each page; then it numbed you - boredom took hold as the full extent of the work instructions, templates, guidelines, checklists and forms started to swell in number, filling your vision and causing you to... panic - sweating now as you surveyed the enormity of what you took for a simple task which had now turned into a complex and byzantine sequence of steps which led you inexorably to the next stage of the toxin's progress: amnesia - why were you here, what was it you wanted to achieve again? And did it matter? Finally, and fatally, you would succumb - either follow the documented process slavishly and submissively until your soul was lost, along with all hope; or abandon the enterprise - nothing was worth this. Whichever course you chose, Bryan's victory was assured and complete. The process had won; he had won. You were collateral damage in the war on human error. Bryan Metcalfe had weaponised bureaucracy.

He also had no time for stupidity. People were so stupid - he wondered how they could stand it. He knew he couldn't. But it was because there was so much stupidity in the world that he had found his niche and built a career on it - so there was that bright spot. Until the bastards had told him he was surplus to requirements. But up until that fateful day he had been a quality ninja - a black-cloaked assassin in the dark arts of quality management. An inventive armoury at his disposal: he could cuff you in process, throttle you in triplicate, drown you in templates, kill you with boredom. All weapons primed to aim at the stupid.

Take Veronica for instance. Christ, was she stupid. Sitting bolt upright at his desk, he forced himself to push on and read through items 14 through 29 of the last

Walkerburn Allotment Group minutes and check that Veronica hadn't made any silly mistakes. Like last time.

Or the time before.

It seemed to Bryan that Veronica was always making mistakes and he had the unenviable job of correcting them for her. Everyone made mistakes, it appeared. Everyone except his good self. And when people made mistakes you either had to accept them, ignore them or correct them. There was no bloody point showing people where they'd gone wrong - he'd learnt that long ago, working thirty-five years for the SSEB.

There were three kinds of people in the world, as far as Bryan was concerned: fools, wastrels and him. Fools made mistakes and couldn't work out how to correct them, or avoid them, and most couldn't understand basic instruction unless it was written out for them in painful detail; wastrels didn't care: usually clock-watchers and time-servers who had adorned the SSEB like useless charms dangling off an enormous bracelet, they were slovenly and did the minimum necessary to earn their money. What did they care if something went wrong? Didn't matter; nobody died. And then there was him: corrector-in-chief and instructor-par-excellence. Bryan wanted to crack on! Do a good job, be as efficient and effective as possible, minimum waste and everyone marching in lockstep towards a common goal. What was wrong with people? Oh he'd long ago given up trying to work that out. Another waste of his time and energy. Far more sensible and efficient to spend the time preventing mistakes in the first place, rather than dealing with the fallout from them. And how did you prevent mistakes? By creating detailed work instructions, procedures, templates and checklists and putting staff - all of them - through the appropriate training so that they were familiar with what was required of them. And then testing them on their knowledge. And repeating the training and testing until it was second nature. And then employing others to supervise and monitor the staff at close quarters to avoid mistakes. And finally developing metrics and key performance indicators to focus people's minds on what was important and what had to be achieved.

Bryan had loved it! The intricacy, the complexity, the exquisite attention to detail. It was a constant war of attrition, a battle against the creativity of stupid people. It was quite remarkable how, despite their stupidity - or maybe because of it - people never failed to find new and innovative ways to screw things up. They could find exciting new ways to find ambiguity where there was none, challenge orthodoxy on how to incorrectly fill out a form, invent completely new methods of working around basic procedures. If there was opportunity for error, these folk would somehow sniff it out - it was like the Chitty Chitty Bang Bang childcatcher in reverse: he was trying to remove the entire possibility for imperfection whilst searching for the slightest trace of it, and all the time the rest of the population were dancing around, playfully, goading him with their disregard and slovenly actions. Open any window for error and into it they would step. Today's Exhibit A: Veronica.

Look! Here and here and here - typos, missing articles, (whisper it) an aberrant apostrophe, and a flagrantly unnecessary carriage return in the middle of a paragraph which led to a premature page throw which put his template out of whack. For God's Sake, Veronica! He shook his head wearily and flicked through the remaining pages. Sometimes it was actually easier and quicker to just do it yourself. Sometimes, working out what was wrong, highlighting it and then explaining it and then waiting for the corrections to come back for reinspection - sometimes, something was so wrong, so off-kilter, that it was easier and cleaner to just throw it away and start again from scratch. He was sorely tempted to re-type this whole thing for her and send his minutes back as hers. But time was short, and his rheumatism was getting worse. He needed a break and a joint and that, he knew, would put paid to his attention to detail for the evening.

Sighing, he quickly typed out a reply to Veronica pointing out, as politely as he could manage, the errors he had found and requesting a corrected copy as soon as possible. The next meeting was later in the week and he needed multiple copies printing ready beforehand.

Message sent, he turned his attention to the manila folder beside him. Half-an-inch thick it contained the papers and proposals for whatever stuff was currently being proposed by the Walkerburn & District Community Council on which he, Bryan Alexander Metcalfe, had been elected to serve. He glanced up at his mantelpiece where he had framed a cutting from the front page of last year's Peeblesshire News showing him, face beaming over a lemon lambswool V-neck, shaking hands with the leader of the council. He smiled now only to grimace as another twinge shot up his right side.

Right. Bugger that for now. Time for that joint.

THREE

Sitting on a promontory overlooking a lazy bend in the barrelling Tweed, something wasn't right and Cullen could smell it. Paul was an old friend but there were limits, especially where drugs were concerned. They had first met when Paul's then-wife had been blackmailed by a sleazy dentist (one of many such married women) and Cullen had arranged for the man to be taught a lesson. Paul had turned up late, as usual, and missed the event but they had shared something, briefly, and Cullen recognised a helpful hand when he saw one.

That had been years ago now but, in all that time, Paul had only ever been an open book. A large print book with a few pages missing and not a lot of big words in it, but an open book nevertheless. Plus he was usually more up-front than Cullen ever appreciated, sometimes uncomfortably so, so not only was his current behaviour suspicious in and of itself, it was also suspiciously out of the ordinary.

What was he up to and why was he being so evasive?

And there was something else nagging him, a small terrier worrying a loose end somewhere in the back of his mind. It wouldn't let go but he couldn't seem to loosen it further and bring it into the light. At times like these, Cullen needed to calm his thoughts and allow his subconscious to snuffle out, blinking. And, at times like these, he felt the need to walk. Somewhere and nowhere.

Anywhere where putting one foot in front of the other would send his mind to sleep and let ideas and decisions solidify.

He took a deep breath, clamped his hat further down onto his head, and let the damp scent of pine needles from Elibank forest engulf him as he set off towards Walkerburn.

Bryan woke up in his armchair, bleary and stiff but pain-free. His journey from cardigan-wearing, strait-laced, drug-averse, upstanding pillar of the community to cardigan-wearing, street-wise, Cannabis-dealing businessman had been a long one but, with his steadfast application and calm practicality, he had ensured it had been almost entirely drama-free and uneventful. Apart from an initial altercation with that doped-out Catweazel, Dominic, who had at first represented his local competition and now comprised his middle-management tier responsible for distribution and customer relations.

It had started with the rheumatism.

No, that wasn't right. It had started with his divorce.

No, actually it had all started with his redundancy. Those bastards.

Bryan didn't resort to foul language often, but he was unable to contemplate this final chapter of his life without insisting on the *bastards* label for the bastards who had made him bastard redundant.

He hadn't seen it coming. Thirty-five years working for the SSEB, he had his retirement and full-pension entitlement in his sights when the wheels suddenly and dramatically came off his life and he skidded wildly off the even surface of his existence and ended up neck-deep in a septic tank. When he emerged blinking nine months later he was divorced, essentially unemployable and desperately short of money.

Which was when life rang the doorbell one final time, knifed him in the stomach and thrust a package of full-blown rheumatoid arthritis in his hands and marched off. Bryan remembered distinctly sitting in his armchair one evening, aching all over as the darkness fell around him and he was too much in pain to get up and turn the lights on. The gloom grew and the rain started to hammer at the windows, his joints echoing every beat on the glass, and realised that no-one was going to help him unless he helped himself.

The next morning, pain keeping him awake, he had made his way down to his allotment, barely even light, to attempt some calming garden therapy when there had been a fire. Just a small one, probably started by some kids messing about the night before. The shed on the allotment next to his was smouldering, presumably too damp to actually catch light, and no-one else was around that early so he stole over the ramshackle fence which separated these two patches of ground: his all trim and neat, bamboo canes and trellis subdividing his own square footage precisely and prettily; his anonymous neighbour's a riot of overgrown grass, wild-headed weeds and thistles. Peering into the dirty broken window he could see a rickety arrangement of metal shelves bearing plant pots containing nothing but shrivelled foliage. The padlock on the shed door had been freed so he prised the ragged-bottomed door open, doused the smoking pile of rags in the corner and inspected the interior further. There had clearly been some attempt at a camp-fire inside the shed, empty cans of Special Brew and a large bottle of Extra-strong cider lay discarded in a heap off to one side, and lying on the windowsill, so clean and pristine that it stood out starkly against the smoke-discoloured and cobwebbed interior, was an emaciated rolled tube of pure white paper with a few wisps of green showing at one end, the other neatly twisted to a close. A beacon. A sign, calling him, beckoning him. It was, Bryan understood immediately, a cannabis cigarette. What he would later come to refer to as, variously, a joint, a spliff, a reefer or a doobie.

Words which, back then, were largely unfamiliar territory to Bryan. But later that morning, after extinguishing the fire, tidying up his neighbour's shed as best he could, he had returned home and scoured the internet for information. And the clouds had parted, the pain had lifted from his heart and his eyes surged in his head when he realised that cannabis was not only a widely-effective relief from rheumatic pain but, if grown in quantities, it would prove a very lucrative money supply.

He had started in his spare room, terrified that he would be discovered. He bought containers and lights, heaters and seeds, books and shielding, and built himself a small but effective growing room at the cost of only a few hundred pounds. Calmly and methodically he set about creating a system. Through trial and error and an empirical approach he learnt what worked and what didn't, documented it all (naturally) and ended up with a model he could replicate over and over - even franchise if he'd been brave (or foolish) enough to allow other people to get involved in the enterprise.

And his idea for where he was going to replicate this growing facility? It was, he felt, genius. He would use abandoned or disused sheds on the allotment site. There were already a few, like the one which had been used as a makeshift campsite. But Bryan wanted reliability, security, safety. He couldn't have vandals breaking in and finding his plants - or worse, stealing them. So he had a vested interest in there not being any sheds which looked derelict or shabby or easy to enter. Everything had to look well-used and cared for.

Plus growing rooms needed to be secure, draft-free, well-lit, warm. Which would require power.

So he set about becoming the master of the allotment group. Professionally and consistently, Bryan started volunteering. Turning up at committee meetings, offering to take on tasks others found tiresome, eventually being voted into the committee and later being voted Chairman. He was a natural, everybody said so. And all the time he was skilfully manoeuvring himself into a position of control and authority, he was drafting new rules and procedures for the committee - processes which would allow him control over unused plots, giving him unique access to them until they were reallocated to new owners - and an approach which formalised, slowed and sclerotised everything under a weight of red tape. After just a year Bryan had fashioned the WAG into a child of his own design, with himself supreme in name and deed, able to use an increasing number of plots to grow cannabis and bring him extra money which was, at first, much-needed and later much-appreciated if no longer required.

And.

And, and, and. The *piece de resistance,* the icing on the bastard cake, was that he was able to route power to each of his growing sheds by tapping into existing electricity supplies of properties that skirted the edges of the allotment ground. Here a tap, there a tap. He well knew how to do this, safely and essentially undetected. His years at the SSEB sprung freshly back to mind and he revelled in this power - literally - he could now so easily acquire. It was almost too easy! If he needed another room, he could click his fingers and make one happen, hook it up to power and voila - his empire had grown another arm. And those bastards at what was-now Scottish Power? Yeah, let them suffer. He was stealing *their* electricity, and therefore, *their* money. No-one else was hurt in the process, no-one else affected. The homes around the allotment ground were none the wiser at this tapping of unmetered electricity and as long as no-one pried too closely at the manicured allotments with their pristine sheds with blacked-out windows.... Even if they did, during the day there was nothing to give away the fact that cannabis was growing in half a dozen unconnected sheds. It was only at night that there might be a detectible leak of light from a insufficiently blacked-out window, or the shimmer of a heat haze in the cold night air.

But, when all was said and done, who on earth would go prowling around an allotment ground? In Walkerburn? At night?

Sitting in the kitchen, breathing the deep sigh of satisfaction that can only come from having devoured a steaming full-cooked breakfast at the start of your day and knowing that it would keep you going until... well, for as long as you wanted generally. Paul pushed the empty plate away and sat back in the chair. The sun was peering out from behind a bank of unspectacular clouds and blessing the allotment ground with light and shadow. It was a bucolic scene, sedate and end-of-summer sweet and Paul wondered once more whether having an allotment would be something for him and Shirl to aim for: a shared endeavour which they could enjoy together while communing with their fellow Walkerburners.

Nah. He'd hate it. But she'd love it.

Paul had had relationships before. Even been married once. But Shirley was different, somehow. Something about it felt real and honest and true and he knew, when he looked back at his past relationships, there had been times - plenty of them - when he had upset his then-partner, or later found out he had, and he had tried earnestly and genuinely to learn from these occasions and not repeat them. Shirley somehow fitted a Shirley-shaped hole inside him - a hole he hadn't realised he had until she came along and slid right in, like she'd belonged there all along, like it had been made for her. Now here she was, and here they were, and he didn't want to fuck it up. Desperately didn't want to fuck it up. So, as was Paul's wont, at the times of most need came the occasion of least thought. Over-thinking would do it every time for Paul and the fear and desperation caused him to think like he'd never had to think before. And thinking wasn't what Paul did well.

Drinking - that was what Paul did well. Putting it away, as folk called it. Actually didn't matter if folk were talking about drink or food, no matter which it was, no matter how much there was of it, Paul excelled at putting it away. And here he sat, thoughtfully for once, contemplating the yield curve of his stomach as it formed a crescent arching away from him, his crotch no longer visible from a sitting position. When had that started, he wondered? It wasn't something he had often considered - Paul was a simple man. He left the contemplation of the infinite, the search for nirvana, the reasoning behind the universe's complex yet beautiful machinery - this he left to others. His metabolism needed all the energy it had to keep up with his food and drink consumption. But finally, at the ripe old age of 49 his body had inventorised his input, totted it up and was now displaying the cost - a long roll of itemised contents, each a price stated in calories and weight gained rather than pounds and pence. Paul surveyed the mental tally, grateful that there was no gratuity added - his belly fat was his own tip.

But back to the thinking. What was he to do? He fondled the burnished tobacco tin in his jacket pocket and drummed it with his fingers. This was what Shirley was looking for. She had glimpsed it somehow - or inferred its existence - and was now like some demonic bloodhound on a trail. And he, like some kind of panicking, guilt-ridden teenager trying not to be caught smoking by his Mum, was frantically snatching the tin from one hiding place and squirrelling it away in another until his racing fear calculated that it would soon be found, whereupon he snatched it back and tormented himself trying to identify a better one.

It was only when Shirley had gone to work that he felt he could relax. Facing the day on his own he could breathe easy and give himself time to work out a solution. How could it be so bloody hard? It seemed that the smaller the item, the more difficult it was to hide rather than less. If it had been some big bloody box perhaps he could have hidden it in plain sight, but this blasted shiny tin? And now Cullen wouldn't help him. Some friend he was. Shirley was relentless in her search, like the Terminator, it seemed to be what she did, all she did, and she absolutely would not stop until she had found it. What the hell was he going to do?

He spent a minute or two scanning the allotments: a few elderly men were up and hard at work already, hoeing and weeding and waving over to their fellow gardeners inviting them for a cup of tea in their own little shed. One woman in a floral headscarf and her slippers still on, was pottering along a little gravel path in her own allotment, deadheading flowers and pruning a collection of very small fruit trees. Elsewhere the small, primly perimetered sections were lying empty, lying prettily in the sunshine. A lone few looked forlorn, their owners absent or forgetful perhaps, the greenery more like brownery, the undergrowth now overgrowth; the sheds neglected, wearing the look of unhappy schoolkids wearing badly-fitting PE kit last to be picked.

Now wait a minute! Paul's eyes lit up. Once again, the soup had spoken. He unconsciously grinned to himself and then somehow, unbidden, he could suddenly hear Cullen's voice in his head - and it was most unwelcome. Paul flinched.

"What are you up to?" Cullen said.

"Nothing."

"Doesn't seem like nothing. You're scared."

"Nope. Not me." Paul was all innocence.

"What are you afraid of?"

"I told you, I'm not."

"Come on. You can tell me. I'm you."

"Right." Paul snorted. "If you're me, you must already know mustn't you?"

"But I want you to tell me. Say it out loud."

"You're weird."

"Come on. What are you afraid of?"

Paul took a long, slow deep breath. "Consequences."

"Ah."

Paul shifted uneasily in his seat. "See those allotments out of the window? Loads of sheds, not many folk around."

"I see them."

"Would make a nice, safe hiding place, wouldn't they? No-one would know, no-one would suspect. Hiding in plain sight! Who's going to break into sheds on an allotment?"

"Well you obviously."

"Apart from me."

"Me?"

Paul's eyes wheeled in his head. What was he hearing? "Why would you break in?"

"To see what you're hiding."

Paul shook his head in sad disbelief. "Why are you so interested? You're as bad as Shirley."

"What do you have to hide?"

"Nothing!"

"Why do you feel guilty then?"

"I don't."

"Really?" Cullen's voice dropped slightly. "Then why are you hearing my voice in your head when I'm not here?"

"Beats me." Paul sulked. "I'd much rather not, if it's all the same to you."

"Ha!" Cullen laughed. Cullen never laughed. Paul grew increasingly concerned at his mental state but the voice inside him pushed on. "It is up to you. You don't need my permission. I'm not here, remember?"

Paul swallowed deliberately, closed his eyes tight and tried to breathe slowly for a minute. Silence. He opened his eyes again, expecting to see something different but he was still sitting at the kitchen counter staring out of the window.

"Boo!" Paul nearly fell off his stool.

"What did you do that for?"

"Checking to see if you're still guilty."

"I'm not." Paul bridled and decided to try going on the attack. "Why is this any of your business?"

"Something is not right."

"Yeah?"

"Yes." Cullen paused and Paul waited. "I can smell it."

"Oh, sorry about that." Paul reddened. "Look, I don't have anything to hide. Not from you."

"I don't believe you."

"Yeah, I'm getting that." Paul was annoyed at being unable to steer this conversation. It was like having a real conversation with his friend, and they never went the way he wanted, or hoped, either. This was ridiculous. "Why?"

"I have my suspicions."

"Unfounded."

"We'll see."

"Well, good luck with that."

"I don't need luck." And Cullen's voice snicked off.

FOUR

It was night and Paul couldn't sleep. His foot was bothering him, his mind was busying itself with this idea of trying to hide his tin in one of the allotment sheds, and then there was this mystery of who was hooked up to Keith's electricity supply, and why. It was not relaxing and eventually he gave up trying to sleep. If he wasn't going to get any rest he might as well strike while the wossname was hot. He just needed a torch - Shirley kept one under the kitchen sink.

She was snoring gently beside him, facing the wall. If he was quiet and careful he could escape without waking her. He scooped his clothes up from his floordrobe by the side of the bed and hunched gingerly out of the bedroom.

Out in the crisp night air, Paul ranged the torchlight over the array of sheds skulking in the darkness. The night was thick and heavy with a watery moon casting a little light over the allotments, silhouetting them against the houses behind. There were a lot of sheds out there. Where to start?

The first one he stole up to was locked but using the torch he could see through the grimy windows that it contained gardening tools, a workbench and a deckchair. The second and third were also clearly sheds in regular use.

The fourth, though, struck a chord with him immediately. The windows were covered up with newspaper painted black.

"Why would anyone blackout the contents of an allotment shed?" said a voice in the blackness.

"Not you again." Paul sneered at Cullen's voice in his head, then his heart shot into his throat and he leapt back letting out an involuntarily "Fucking Hell!"

The man himself was leaning calmly against the corner of the shed, arms folded, his leather cowboy hat casually askew.

"What the fuck are you doing here? You scared the bejesus out of me!"

Cullen ignored him and repeated his question: "Why would anyone blackout the windows of an allotment shed?"

"Duh. So you can't see inside."

"And why don't you want anyone to see inside?"

"Tramps?" Paul said, scanning the allotment ground as if the very word could bring a horde of them clamouring into the space.

"Or..." Cullen raised his eyebrows and looked coolly at his friend. "Covering up some illegal activity."

"Why do you say that?"

"'Cos it's warm. Can't you feel it?"

Paul raised his hand to a few inches from the shed window, able to feel the heat without even touching it. "Yeah."

"Yeah. So, what do you think might be inside?"

Paul shone his torch directly into Cullen's face, who winced. Paul lowered it slightly so it still illuminated his friend's face.

"What are you doing here?"

"I could ask you the same question."

"I asked first."

"Yes, you did."

"So answer me then!" Paul scowled and waited. Eventually Cullen spoke.

"Spying on you."

"What! Why?"

"Because you're up to something and I wanted to find out what it was."

"And you thought you'd find the answer in the middle of Walkerburn allotments in the bloody dark?"

Cullen smiled. "Looks like that was a good call, doesn't it?"

"And anyway, I'm not up to anything!" Paul protested.

"No? Let's see. Prowling furtively around allotments - "

"With a torch! Not furtive."

"In the middle of the night? When no-one's around? Furtive."

"Could be my own allotment."

"Yeah. The only reason you would tend an allotment would be if scientists had invented a way to grow bacon from seed. Not really you, is it, veg?"

"Could be Shirley's."

"Could be." Cullen considered. "But isn't."

"So what am I doing here then?"

"Only one way to find out." Cullen slipped to his knees with practiced ease. "Train that light on here."

Within seconds the padlock on the hasp was undone. Cullen stood and drew back the door. There was a small number 19 on it.

Light and heat flooded the pair as they stood shielding their eyes from the glare and sudden brightness that stood before them. Inside the shed was a forest of heavy-fronded plants, several feet tall, arranged in dense rows. All were potted in a lattice of deep pots, a matrix of clear plastic tubes ribboning across them, irrigating the soil. Above them and on all sides was LED lighting suspended on thin wires cobwebbing across the shed, their brilliance amplified by aluminium foil lining all internal surfaces, reflecting light and heat everywhere. Three standing heaters emitted an orange glow, radiating a gorgeous warmth out into the cold air.

"What's that?" Cullen pointed to a large cube draped with black material suspended above a humidifier humming in one corner. Paul strode over and pulled the fabric back to reveal an extensive wire frame, inside which were a number of hanging bouquets of leaves. A heavy scent instantly bathed the shed interior.

"Drying rack. Phew!"

"Your allotment you say?" Cullen's eyes narrowed.

"No. Absolutely not. Nope. No way." Paul shook his head as if trying to expel associated guilt through centrifugal force.

"You know what this is, though?"

"Oh aye. Weed."

"Weed?"

"Cannabis, you know. Weed, grass, pot." Paul rattled off.

"You mean drugs." Cullen face was a granite frown. "Strange isn't it, how many slang names for cannabis are gardening words."

"They're not mine." Paul held both palms up, not easy while trying to keep hold of his torch.

"But you knew this would be here?"

"No."

"And you came out in the middle of the night hoping to find it because...?"

"I didn't know it was here!"

"Hmm." Cullen looked sceptical. "What are you doing here then?"

"Um." Paul weighed up his words carefully. "Looking. For a friend."

"This... friend? Does he have a history of drug use? Of secreting illegal substances in other friend's caravans?"

"Oh, these aren't his drugs."

"No? Whose are they then?"

"Well." Said Paul, sucking his teeth. "I think I can take a guess."

"Go on, then."

So Paul did, unburdening himself of Keith's story while Cullen listened intently. By the time he'd finished it seemed Cullen's belief in Paul's guilt had been, at least partially, assuaged.

"So this Metcalfe bloke. Keeping a number of allotments back, not just one. A few."

"'Swhat Keith said."

"So there could be more sheds like this?"

"Aye. I guess."

"It would follow." Cullen looked deep into Paul's eyes. "And, if there are, it would also signify - to me, at least - that this was an almost industrial but certainly commercial operation."

Paul didn't follow his friend's reasoning. "Which means...?"

"Which means you'd be off the hook." Cullen pulled at the tip of his nose, contemplating. "Growing stuff for personal use? I can see that. Running a commercial operation? Not so much."

"Thanks very much for the vote of confidence!" Paul was affronted. "I'm self-employed you know."

"Only because no-one else will employ you."

"Hey!"

"Let's find the others."

"Now?" Paul was enjoying the warmth, and smell, of the shed and not keen on leaving it for the icy darkness around them and an expedition to find an unknown number of other sheds like this. "But how many are we looking for? There's dozens out here. It'll be like playing bloody battleships!"

"Every one we find will make me more and more convinced that you are an innocent man." Cullen raised his eyebrows and waited.

"Good." Paul gave a crisp nod. "I think I'll just stay here while you search. Stand guard on all this lot. 'Case anyone turns up."

Cullen looked at him askance. "I mean, innocent of this. Not innocent, period."

Reluctantly, he took the torch from Paul and padded out across the allotment ground. It was thirty minutes before he returned.

"Nine." Cullen tallied. "And if they're all like this one, that's a huge amount of electricity."

"Aye. Shedloads!" Paul grinned.

The joke didn't register with his friend who was clearly pondering something else. "So it would imply that Mr Metcalfe is actually tapping into more than just your friend's electricity supply. Maybe even one property tap per shed."

Paul whistled softly. "Well, Keith's tap looked like an expert had done it. Almost. But certainly not someone's first attempt."

Cullen looked up at him. "Almost?"

"Well, yeah. See, this tap - it's on the wrong side of the meter. If he'd put the spur on the supply side of the meter then he'd be stealing the electricity invisibly. It wouldn't hit the meter and Keith wouldn't have been charged for it. If they're all like that..."

"And if he'd done them your way, no-one would have found out." Cullen marvelled. "He would have got away with it."

"Well, unless the Electricity people noticed it but... not likely, really."

Cullen thought for a moment. "I'm going to need a pair of overalls, a hi-vis jacket, a hardhat and a clipboard." He handed Paul back his torch.

"Er. OK. I've got all that in my van." Paul considered. "I can get you them tomorrow."

"Are the overalls clean?"

Paul scrunched his nose. "Ish. What do you need 'em for?"

But Cullen had gone.

Paul waited for five clear minutes, keeping a watchful eye out into the cold night air. Once he was happy that Cullen wasn't likely to magically reappear he turned back into shed #19 and bathed once again in the glorious warmth and smell.

Here was a gift from God; a taste of his beloved soup talking. Not only did he now have access to a free supply of hash to keep him mellow for, well, quite some considerable time; and it was right on his - alright, Shirl's, same thing - doorstep. He could pop out every night, just like this, bathe in the warmth and light a rollie. But better yet - the croutons on his soup de jour - was this was a brilliant hiding place! The perfect spot had been under his nose this entire time. He cast around the shed for a handy nook or other hiding place, settling on a satisfyingly loose floorboard which gave access to a patch of dry earth below. Carefully he wrapped his burnished tin in a spare piece of the black fabric that was lying on the windowsill and reverentially deposited this prize into its now sacred space. He finished the concealment by brushing some dust and soil from the corner of the shed over the moved floorboard to make it blend it with its bedfellows.

Happy with the overall effect, he wiped the dirt from his hands on his trousers and reached into his pocket for a packet of Rizlas.

June wiped her hands on her pinnie when she heard the doorbell and, stiffened with indignation, strode to the door to give the delivery man a piece of her mind. Four hours she'd been waiting - four bloody hours! What was the point of them giving her a delivery window and then ignoring it? She had a spare bedroom full of dirty washing she couldn't shift and a knackered machine in her kitchen she needed shut of.

"Well, about time too! I've ..." She blinked, confused, at the tall man in hi-vis with a clipboard, curly hair trying hard to escape from beneath his hardhat. The man was smiling strangely at her, as if he was unfamiliar with that particular expression. "Oh, sorry." She recovered herself, although not before looking behind the man for signs of two non-existent burly delivery men. "I was expecting-"

"Scottish Power!" The man waved a laminated card in her face for a micro-second and then officiously clicked the end of his ballpoint.

"Oh, no thanks." June smiled weakly. "We're with Bulb."

"I'm sorry?"

"Bulb. Not long changed actually. Anything to try and

cut down the bills. It's atrocious!"

"Bulb?"

"Aye. I think they're new. Not been going long any road. It's a right palaver innit? Bet you can't keep up, all these new energy suppliers. Used to be simple in my day. Yours too I imagine?"

"Aye. Well. But I'm not here to ask you to switch supplier."

"Oh."

"No, see Scottish Power - yes, we do supply people's electricity. And gas. But we are also responsible for the distribution network, regardless of your supplier. I'd like to ask you a few questions, if you don't mind?"

June looked up and down the street, in vain, seeking signs of the missing delivery van, and let out a huge snort of frustration. "Go on, then. But be quick. Soon as you're gone I'm going to phone these blooming delivery people and see what they're playing at!"

"Sorry. Mrs, erm...?"

"Campbell."

"Right, Mrs Campbell. Can I ask you if there has been any noticeable change in your electricity bills - up or down - recently?"

"Down! You must be bloody joking!" June crossed her arms and noticed the hairs on them had risen. "Do you know how much we pay to heat this place? I mean, I know electric's not supposed to be as efficient as gas - not that we've got the money to go splashing around converting from one to the other, you understand. Chance'd be a fine thing. But bloody hell! I know we're on the Economy tariff and everything but it used to be around £100 a month - all-in. Now it's often double or even triple that. Got a bill at the end of the winter months, nearly seven hundred quid they wanted! This is a maisonette, not bloody Tynecastle! My Charlie went through the roof! I had 'em on the phone day in, day out, trying to get to the bottom of it. Sent 'em photos of the meter reading. Took a wee video, actually, of the numbers whirring round. Sent 'em that. Did they bother their arses to come round?"

"No?" The man ventured.

"Of course, bloody not! They'll take your money soon as look at you but when you want some back 'cos summat's not right, different story isn't it? Beggars they are! Absolute beggars. My Charlie's got a worse word for them but then he used to work down the coalboard."

"Right. And you say this, erm, price-jump happened... last winter?"

June thought for a moment. Cullen, for it was he, appreciated the brief silence.

"Yes. Around then. And they haven't got any lower since! And I'll tell you something else for nothing- Oh, there they are!" June's attention was caught immediately by a bright yellow lorry which had turned the corner into her road. One scruffy youngster emerged from the passenger side as the vehicle pulled up at the kerb.

"About time!" June yelled at the callow, acned soul. "Where the bloody hell have you been? I've been waiting in all bloody day-"

"Right, Mrs Campbell. I think I have everything..."

June dismissed the man with a irritated wave of her hand, his questions forgotten. The target of her frustrations had finally arrived.

Cullen was glad of the chance to retreat down the path and away from the delivery driver coming to the defence of his young assistant, currently weathering a mighty onslaught from June Campbell. Glancing at his watch he realised it was past 5pm and he had now visited all the houses that bordered the allotment grounds. He turned a corner at the end of the road and into a short stretch of woodland bordering the river, stopped to remove his jacket, overalls and hardhat and dropped them in a nearby bin.

"Eleven?" Paul gave a low whistle. "Are you sure?"

"Yes. Might be more in fact - two doorbells didn't answer."

"But you only found nine warm sheds."

"Aye." Cullen considered this for a moment. "Maybe he's getting ready to set up another two. Or maybe he used to have eleven and two are lying fallow. Do you use crop rotation in cannabis farming? "

"How would I know?" Paul said, offended at the implication.

"Anyway. Eleven's enough wouldn't you say?"

"Enough for what?"

"For what I have in mind." Cullen's eyes narrowed.

"What have I told you about sharing your plans with other people? And, by other people, I - of course - mean me."

"This is eleven properties whose electricity bills have soared over the past twelve months." Cullen waggled the piece of paper from the clipboard at Paul. "Why don't you, and your similarly tapped friend, go check out and see which sheds are connected to which property. Check that they've all been tapped?"

"Why me?"

"Because you're the electrical supply expert, n'est-ce pas?"

"Harrumph." Paul grudgingly took the sheet of paper from Cullen. "And if they have?"

"Oh, I'm sure they have."

"What then?"

"We'll see." Cullen smiled. "First, I'm going to pay a visit to Mr Metcalfe."

"OK. Can I have my clipboard back?" Cullen tossed him the clipboard and Paul reattached the paper to it and scanned down the list of names and addresses. "Where's my hardhat, jacket and overalls by the way?"

Cullen blinked, remembering. "Ah."

"Mr Metcalfe?"

"Yes?" Bryan had his door on the safety chain, peering out at this man wearing a tatty green waterproof coat, a rain-soaked leather cowboy hat and several day's worth of stubble. It was dusk and Bryan had no intentions of taking any chances with someone as scruffily attired as this chap. Safety first, thought Bryan - words to live by.

"Bryan Metcalfe?"

"Councillor Bryan Metcalfe, actually." Bryan bristled, there was something menacing about this man and his strangely quiet manner. "Can I help you?"

"Councillor is it?" The man nodded as if to himself. "Yes, you can help me. I'd like to talk to you about the allotment sheds."

Bryan relaxed, relieved this was probably about some simple administrative issue. He slipped smoothly into bureaucrat smarm. "I'm afraid that, whilst I chair the Walkerburn Allotment Group, I am unable to act alone on any allotment matters - you will have to deal with the committee as a whole, and we don't meet again until tomorrow evening. If it's an allotment you wish to apply for I could give you a form to take away and bring back on Thursday?"

Bryan was closing the door when he found the stranger's foot in the way. He looked up into cold grey, humourless eyes.

"I don't wish to apply." The man's voice was quiet and unhurried, and all the more menacing for it. "I wish to talk to you about the many sheds on the allotment ground which are currently being powered by illegally tapping into the electricity supplies on neighbouring properties."

"I don't know what you're on about." Bryan fought to quell panic rising in his throat. "If you don't get your foot out of my door, I'm calling the police."

"May I wait? I'd like to show them the cannabis farms these power taps are helping to feed."

Bryan's eyes widened in alarm, and then widened further as he fell back under the power of this man who pushed his front door forcefully, causing the frame to splinter as the safety chain anchor gave way.

"Don't want a fracas in the street do we now, Councillor?" The man gave an icy smile and closed the door behind him. Bryan retreated down the hallway, panicking but sticking to his story. He had prepared for even such an unlikely scenario as this. Alright, he hadn't quite imagined it transpiring in this exact manner but he had done a full risk assessment on his operation and was confident all was in place. "I don't know what you're talking about." He managed, wishing he could sound more unworried than he did. "Whilst we, as the allotment group, bear responsibility for the allotment ground as a whole - and their collective operation - we are very much NOT responsible for the activities of individual allotment owners on their own plots. That is entirely up to them, provided they abide by WAG conditions of ownership."

The man was bearing down on Bryan, his shadow looming as he stretched out one finger and prodded Bryan repeatedly in the chest as he found himself backed up against the hall mirror. "These allotments I am talking about - eleven of them, in all - I understand to be under your personal control, as the individual responsible for issuing new plots and managing dormant plots awaiting new owners."

"Ah, ah..." Bryan tried to remain calm, while his brain rappelled from the clifftop of oversight down into the quarry of detail he truly hoped his records would confirm. "I think you'll find that there are no... currently... dormant plots, Mister... ah?"

The man stayed silent, glaring stony-faced. Bryan swallowed hard.

"Ah... I can show you detailed records. Records of all current plots, their owners, dates of ownership transfer, deeds of ownership. Anything you like!" Here Bryan felt a mild rush - the delightful security of terra firma beneath his feet, the conviction that he of all people would have his records straight. "I think, perhaps a mistake has been made?"

"I think so too." The man Cullen held Bryan's gaze. "By you."

"Ah..."

"Show me your records."

"Of course. Of course." Bryan grabbed the hem of his lambswool cardigan and pulled the garment down, smoothly over his paunch. He took a short but deep breath, calming himself. "This way, please. I'm sure we can iron out this little... crease of misunderstanding."

Bryan led the man through to his living room where, up against the fireplace wall, he had a tidy teak bureau. Opening the lid he revealed his old laptop which he turned on and waited. The two men stood awkwardly in the gaping stillness as the ancient machine, with occasional clicks, whirrs and beeps, powered up and hummed into a usable state. After what seemed like weeks, Bryan reached for the keyboard. Pecking out some commands with the index fingers of each hand, he finally pulled up a spreadsheet on screen and opened both palms. "See for yourself."

"Show me." The mad cowboy loomed over the hunched figure of Bryan who obediently scrolled slowly down the sheet.

"See. There are sixty-four plots - each row here is a plot. This column is the number, last date of ownership, owner's name - anything with WAG means it's dormant and awaiting reallocation. As you can see, there are only - what - three dormant ones?"

"Hmm." The man was unconvinced but, it seemed, in the face of black-and-white evidence, at a loss as to how to proceed. Bryan sighed appreciatively and decided to offer a useless olive branch.

"Was there a particular plot number you wanted to look at?"

Silence for a moment. "Number 19."

"19? Let's see." He scrolled back up the screen, found what he was looking for, and then read it out loud. "Current owner: Iain Nesbitt McKenna."

"What?"

Bryan felt something shiver and the hairs rose on the back of his neck. The man's voice had dropped to an icy temperature and the laptop screen seemed to belly out to engulf them both. Bryan daren't look round and he tried to swallow, only to find his mouth dry. He ran his tongue around his mouth to try and generate some saliva only to feel himself spun in his chair, his terrified face meeting a mask of stone. "Say that name again."

"Ah... Iain McKenna." Bryan suddenly wanted to cry. He had never been so afraid in his life - this man with a voice of death standing beside him, instructing him to repeat words which seemed harmless enough but clearly had some significance he did not understand.

"Nesbitt. Iain Nesbitt McKenna, you said."

"Yes. Yes, that's right. That's what it says."

The man grabbed Bryan by the neck and squeezed. "Give me everything you have on this man."

"But ... that's all I have!" Bryan struggled for breath. "I've only been chairman for a year or so. These are all my records, on computer. I don't have anything else. Just this!"

"Address?"

"Erm..." Bryan turned back to the screen and tabbed right. "None." He said in despair.

"Contact number, next of kin. Anything?"

"No. Nothing." Bryan scrabbled left and right in his sheet, clicked randomly on other tabs suddenly blinded by fear, his carefully curated records an impenetrable unfamiliar landscape which now held him, lost. He felt a tear roll down his cheek and whirled around to look at his persecutor's face, for perhaps one final time. "Who is he?"

The cowboy wore a glazed look, staring through him and Bryan could see his question hadn't registered. He tried again.

"Who's Iain McKenna? What's this all about? I thought this was about allotments and electricity and that!"

His eyes slowly focussing back, the man's voice crushed Bryan's heart: "It was."

FIVE

"Bollocking bastard!" Keith spat. "I knew that fecker was up to something. When I get my hands on him..." He left the sentence unfinished but Paul could see Keith's fury flashing in his eyes. There would be a reckoning for Bryan Metcalfe.

"Well, let's see where this first tap goes shall we?"

"What about mine?"

"We'll get to yours. Orders is orders." Paul waved the clipboard.

"Whose orders."

"Never mind. Come on."

The meters for these terraced properties of flats and maisonettes were arranged in clusters of four and six in separate cabinets at the rear of the buildings, all giving straight onto the allotment ground. Paul could see what a simple operation this would have been - little chance of being caught red-handed doing the tap, and little chance of detection once they were in place. Metcalfe had done a very neat and tidy job here, Paul was impressed. The cable from each tap was tacked down on the cabinet walls and chased down through the base into a shared corrugated plastic tube. This was buried under an inch or so of packed gravel and Paul soon lost its trail. He wandered over to the chainlink fence which marked the edge of the allotment ground and started pulling back undergrowth, kicking at the soil beneath the fence for signs of the tubed cable.

"Well, it must run under the fence and then split out again to reach each separate shed." Paul stood and looked through the mesh of the fence out over the now-empty allotments. A varied arrangement of rectangular plots, edged here with planks buried end-on, there with expanses of trellis or low wooden fences. One even had a wee gate into it. Not all the allotments contained a shed, but most did. "Let's see if we can trace them from the sheds back to the meters."

They walked down a wide path until, level with the back of the gardens of the houses either side, it opened out into the large allotment space. From this angle, and in the daylight with no metal fence separating him from it, the place looked huge to Paul.

"Wow. How many allotments are there?"

"Sixty-four." Keith said authoritatively. "Eleven of 'em idle apparently - courtesy of B Metcalfe, arse of this parish." They wandered down a central pathway into the centre of the multi-sectioned site. "You know, plenty of folk wait years for an allotment to come up. Albert MacIntyre died last month, been waiting nine months for one to come free - never got one."

"How old was he?"

"No idea. Old guy. Not too steady on his pins, old Albert."

"How would he have managed one of these then?" Paul spread one arm across three or four plots in front of them. "They're bloody big these aren't they? Bigger than I thought."

"Ten roods." Keith said, his authoritative tone returning.

"Eh?"

"Standard size. Ten roods."

"What the feck's a rood?"

"A rood is a pole. Or a perch. Or a rod - in England. Same thing. They're measurements dating back to Anglo-Saxon times. "

"Like Holyrood?"

"Different type o' rood." Keith winked. "Rood in that case means a cross. Church of the Holy Rood means Church of the Holy Cross." He tapped his right temple. "'S called learning."

"Arse." Paul grimaced but was impressed nevertheless. "You thought of joining our pub quiz team?"

Keith's eyebrows raised. "Oh aye? When's that then?"

"Thursdays. Down the Lamb and Flag."

"Ach, can't do Thursday's. Play five-a-side."

"Ah well. Keep it in mind." Paul said.

They reached shed #19 and Paul started rooting around the base, looking for the entry point for a cable. Keith stood and watched.

"So how much is a rood then?" asked Paul.

"It's a quarter of a chain." Keith winked again.

"Oh fuck off! Sure you don't want to measure them in pecks or bushels?"

"Them's for volume." Keith retorted, as if the very proposal was nonsensical.

"Right. 'Course. That would be stupid, wouldn't it?"

"Aye."

"Not like using some unit of measure from the twenty-first century. Madness!"

Keith grinned at Paul, shaking his head. "Aye been, mate. Aye been."

"Right so, in real money, how long is a rood?"

"Five and a half yards."

"Right. So 55 yards long then?"

"No." Keith smiled but could see Paul was tired of the game. "In allotment terms, rood is short for square rood. So an allotment is about 300 square yards. 250 square meters if you're being European."

"Bloody hell! Tending that's goin' to keep you fit innit?"

"Oh aye."

"Doesn't sound like old Albert would've been up to it."

"Nah, we help each other out here. One big family." Keith clenched his teeth. "With one big bollocking wanker in charge." He screwed up his face and put on a nasal voice. "Bryan with a *y*! Don't forget." He returned his voice to normal. "Fecking knob."

"Knob. Arse. Wanker. Make your mind up - which one is he?"

"All of 'em."

"Ah, now. Can't be having that." Paul raised himself back up from his crouch and began kicking the ground idly, meanwhile seizing the opportunity to finally shine some erudition back on Keith. "Me and Davy have, over many long hours and much cogitation, come up with a taxonomy-"

"A what now?"

"Taxonomy. System of classification." Paul beamed. "Actually it was Scott's idea but, doesn't matter. Detail. And within that we have a ranking scheme."

"Why?"

"Duh." Paul looked shocked. "So that words like *arse* and *wanker* can be used accurately, in their proper context, and not thrown around willy-nilly like so much chaff. It's called the Swearword Hierarchy/Insult Taxonomy - SH/IT for short."

"Go on then." Keith waved an invisible cloak to the ground in front of Paul. "Enlighten me."

"Right, well. I can't remember the whole thing right now - Davy's the official record on this - but I can give you some highlights."

"As you wish."

"Ok. So, first, all the trivial, polite insults: *moron, twerp, idiot, tit* and so on? Forget about them - there's a big long list and no-one really uses them much anymore. Insult inflation. Same for *shit, shithead, bullshit,* and all those. Leave them to the Americans. - give them something - they're just lame. Only the British know how to swear properly."

"Huh." Keith nodded appreciatively.

"Right, then, *arse* and *arsehole* are not the same - *arsehole* is always worse."

"Really?"

"Oh aye." Paul nodded curtly, the point too obvious to pursue.

"Then you've got *knob*, which is worse than *arse* but not as bad as *dick*." Paul started counting off fingers. "Then comes *dickhead*, and then *bellend*, beats all of them."

"Right."

"Ah, here it is." Paul found a single black cable, about half-an-inch thick, leading from one corner of the shed down into the soil. "Now we need to find out which meter this comes from."

"How do we do that?"

"Hmm. Bollocks. How about you go back to the meters and I'll pull on this end and you see if one cable tightens at the other?"

"O...kay." Keith wasn't convinced. "And what about *bollocks*, and any *bollocks*-related ones: *bollock-brain, bollock-breath*, like that?"

"Oh, they're kinda off to one side. Special purpose

usage, Davy calls it. *Bollocks* on its own? Just a utilitarian utterance."

"A utilitarian utterance?" Keith's mouth gaped. "Feck off!"

"Swiss Army Knife kinda word." Paul clarified.

"Well I am fond of that particular one I must say."

"Aye, I noticed." Paul followed on to the fingers on his other hand. "But, you know, like *fuck* - and it's more polite adaptation *feck* - you can stick 'em anywhere in a sentence, even inside a word. Noun, verb, adjective. Ultimate universal tool - except when overdone, obv."

"Oh aye. Obv." Said Keith, now struggling to keep up.

"Then, right at the top, you got your C word. Not a lot of use for that, but gaining traction and becoming more widespread as we speak. Won't be long before it hits the mainstream and then we'll have nowhere left to go. Insult inflation will have run its course and we'll be all out of Anglo-Saxon."

"You forgot *wanker*." Keith noted.

"Ah, right. Yeah well, *wanker*'s off to one side slightly as well I think. There's a whole cluster of *wank*-related ones: *jerk, tosser, wanker, wankstain, cumshot.* Some more I can't remember now. Davy's working on them now. Trying to synthesise them into the whole."

"That another euphemism for wanking? Synthesising into a hole?" Keith grinned and elbowed Paul.

"No." Paul said, straitlaced. "So, to address your insult selection for Bryan Metcalfe - *wanker* beats *knob* which beats *arse*. So, he's a wanker."

"A total wanker."

"An absolute wanker."

"Ooh. How do the adjectives affect the taxonomy?"

"Not sure." Paul frowned. "Another one for Davy."

"Hmmm." Keith said. "When did you say your pub quiz was?"

"Thursdays. Now, get back to the meters and I'll give a tug on this cable."

Bryan awoke, an alarm beeping annoyingly. For a moment he was unsure where he was. He had been in the belly of bad, bad dream. His ex-wife, Doreen, had been hectoring him. Scolding him in his own house and it had all seemed very, very real.

"Where've you been?" Doreen was puce, as if she had been holding her breath the entire time he had been away, building up a head of steam ready to vent the minute he reappeared.

"Out." Bryan stood awkwardly on the mat inside the door, a small bunch of flowers wilting in his hands under her damning gaze. "I'm-"

"I don't want to hear it." Doreen held a hand up and out, directing traffic and putting him on hold. "Don't think you can just apologise and everything will be ok. And don't think you can come crawling back in here with those!" She glared at the sorry bouquet. "It's all too late for that."

Bryan's head spun. This was not the reception he had been expecting. "What... what do you mean?"

"A fine end to a thirty year marriage this is!"

"What?"

"You heard me."

"But Dore!" Bryan appealed for a hearing but it was clear that one was not going to be forthcoming.

"No *but*s, Bryan. I only stayed here until you came back to tell you I'm leaving." Doreen nodded to the suitcases standing in the hallway.

"But where are you going?"

"Never you mind." Doreen snapped. "All you need to know is that you'll be paying for it."

"But there's no money left! That's why I-"

"Tough! Find some."

"How?"

"I don't know and I don't care."

"But-"

"And you'll be needing more to pay for these!" She threw a handful of A4 pages which failed to reach him and fluttered helplessly to his feet. He bent to scoop them up, his eyes starting to tear.

"What are these?" He leafed through them, the digits on the paper reeling, the large red capital letters burrowing into his brain.

"They are what we've been trying to live off these past two years, Bryan. Two years while you have sat on your arse and moaned and failed - failed, completely - to provide for us."

"But I did provide." He tried to protest, his brain fogging up.

"Ha! If you had, I wouldn't have needed to run up these debts would I?"

"Debts?" He muttered, unable to process the information.

"Damn right."

"But I don't understand."

"You stopped earning. We needed money for heating, clothing, food."

"But I gave you an allowance."

"Which wasn't enough. We needed more and I was damned if I was going to go through your bloody reviews and questionnaires in order to increase our budget! You and your stupid-"

"But that's all we could afford!"

"Says who? Says you? You who has no idea and no experience of running a household? But that didn't matter did it? That wasn't up for debate because you were the man in charge weren't you? You were in control. And didn't I bloody know it."

"But we had to live within our means! I was made redundant."

"You were made redundant!" Doreen mimicked, doing a very good impression of his nasal whine. "Christ, don't I bloody know it! Do you have any idea what it's like living 24/7 with an officious know-it-all who demands everything is done by the book?"

"I-"

"Course you don't! Any more than you understand why you were made redundant in the first place. You're a bloody blind fool, Bryan Metcalfe and I can't stand it anymore. You had a steady job, a good salary, a gold-plated pension. And you threw it away."

"How... What...? It wasn't my fault!"

"Of course it was. Whose fault was it?"

"They reorganised! I got made redundant!"

"Yes, you did. And why? They don't make the valuable people redundant. The staff the business rely on. Do they? No, it's the makeweights, the deadwood, the -"

"I was a senior manager!" Bryan interjected, outraged.

"A senior manager." Doreen sneered. "Don't make me laugh. A senior liability."

"It was the new bosses, the new brooms. You don't understand Dore, new bosses coming in want to make their mark, show they are bringing change. Sometimes the fact that there is change - any change - is enough, doesn't matter what the change is. It's capitalism, red in tooth and claw. The markets speaking! Privatisation brings efficiencies, cost-savings, profit!"

"Is that right?" Doreen put her hands on her hips. "And do you think all your processes and procedures, endless checks and double-checks, were all efficiency measures, hmm? Did all these overheads and scrutineers contribute to lower costs?"

"But they were necessary!" Bryan protested. "These new blokes didn't take the time to look at the alternatives, they just swept everything away. Everything I had put in place to make the place function! It was all needed to make sure the stupid staff did their jobs properly!"

"That's right." Doreen's voice was iced velvet. "All the new bosses above you were stupid and all the staff below you were stupid. It was only you that wasn't stupid wasn't it? But look now, all these new bosses they've got jobs. And all your old staff, they've still got jobs. So who's the stupid one, now? Answer me that."

"But-"

"And for the past two years all you've done is make me feel stupid. *Me.* Oh I can see all too clearly how your former work colleagues and staff and bosses must have felt about you. I've had it up to here with your petty rules and pernickety spreadsheets. You are a stupid, self-important, puffed-up little prick Bryan Metcalfe. And you're just too blind to see it. But everyone else can and everyone else has. And they've all abandoned you. Except me. And now it's my turn."

"What?"

"You heard me. I'm leaving. Now let me by." She bustled towards him and Bryan limply stood there, bemused, as she made a show of heaving the suitcases past him and out into the porch.

"Dore!"

"Too late, Bryan. Much too late."

He watched disbelievingly as she wrangled the cases into the boot of his car, snatched the keys from his hand and reversed out of the drive. By the time he had recovered his wits, Doreen had long gone.

It was the *Nesbitt* that had done it for Cullen. That had left no doubt in his mind that he was dealing with *the* Iain McKenna. And the name without the *Nesbitt* was bad enough. How many times in his sleep had he seen those black, hooded, heartless eyes looking at him? The man had haunted his dreams in what felt like a different, earlier life now.

His but not his.

But there had been no further clue at Metcalfe's. And none here either. Here in shed #19 Cullen ripped the lights and heaters from their sockets plunging the interior into darkness. Crying out McKenna's name as if it were a weapon. His violent fingers, grasping and clawing and yanking everything he could, destroying this vile place, its contents and the values it represented, tearing the place apart looking for some lead, some shred of evidence that might lead him closer to the man.

To *her*.

He ripped the paper from the windows, allowing a watery light into this baking prison. Slashing at the plants and pulling them savagely from their roots, before stomping on them and tossing them out into the vanishing day. Metcalfe was irrelevant now. An aging, bureaucratic bungler who had no idea what he had touched, however remotely. He hadn't been worth hurting or torturing for information he didn't have.

So there had to be some lead here in this shed.

Had to be, but wasn't.

The place ransacked, Cullen stood empty and empty-handed. All hope and emotion had been wrung from him and the furious, raging injustice had descended to shroud his vision - a familiar but long-forgotten fog had returned and shrunk his hatred to a laser point. The numbness he had built to keep out the pain and terrible memories, had cracked and splintered - the carefully constructed dam was about to burst under this new blow.

With a hopeless, impotent howl, Cullen set light to the shed and fled, knowing he would be unable to outrun the pain.

"Are you sure about all this?" Geoff asked, his dry, drink-addled face resembling nothing so much as a pot pourri stuffed into a slightly-too-small muslin bag.

Keith ran his finger down the list. "32b - that's you Geoff. You've been paying for the contents of shed #43. 33a - Val - you've been paying for -"

"He's making it up!" Val cried to the assembled throng, then turned back to Keith. "You're making it up!"

"Do you think I'd make something like this up?" Keith snorted, waving the sheet of paper above his head so that everyone could see it. He strained over the hubbub. "Bollocking hell people! How many of you have seen your leccy bill's rocket?"

Everyone's hand shot up. There were twenty people packed into this small room at the back of The George Hotel, many had been drinking and conversation had been lively. It was now threatening to be fractured and inconclusive. Keith had not expected to have to wrestle his audience into submission.

"And now you know why! Metcalfe's been nicking your electricity. All of our electricity. He's been syphoning it off to grow drugs, get himself high, and sell them. He's been making money off *our* money!"

"That's conjecture!" Val again.

"Conjecture? Why are you protecting him, Val? Why don't you believe the facts?"

"Them's not facts! That's just a piece of paper. We can't go making allegations based on your say-so. He's an old man. A councillor! A pillar of the community."

"A pillock of the community." Someone snarked and hoots of laughter shot through the crowd and threatened to set this informal meeting off-balance.

"And if it is true, what can we do? Val's right - he's a councillor." A small voice, Eric, a frail gentleman whose pension had been sorely compromised by his inflated electricity bills.

"What can we do? We can call the police! These are crimes! Theft? Drugs?"

"That won't do anything will it? Masons innit? Police. Council. They're all in on it." Said Eric.

"Am I hearing this right?" Keith was bewildered. Could no-one see sense? He wondered if Metcalfe had put something in the water as well. "Remember what it was like before? Before Bryan-with-a-y Big Bollocks came wading in and took o'er the place with his feckin' points o'order and his agendas an' that? We never had big leccy bills before did we?"

"That's coincidence!" Val piped up again. "And what's wrong with process? Someone needs to make things happen. To make things happen you need a system. Organisation."

"Oh spare me!" Keith ranted. "You think that's what all this was for - keep things organised? Wake up sheep! He was putting all this guff in place to stop new allotments being parcelled out so he could use them to sell drugs! It was all part of his plan. The more allotments weren't in use, the more drugs he could grow, the more money he'd make and the more electricity he'd use!"

Geoff nodded. "We shoulda told him to feck off back to where he came from-"

"Gala." Eric interjected, nodding knowingly.

"And keep his feckin' big city ideas to hisself."

"Not sure you can call Gala a *big city*." Eric again, starting to prove himself a bit of a pain in Keith's arse.

"Look, this is all irrelevant!" Keith spat. "All you need to know is this: he used all these processes and red tape to hold stuff up - all the time using this delay to grow and sell drugs and STEAL OUR LECCY!!!"

This quietened the crowd and many took a pause to take a drink. Keith decided to try and seal the deal with one last push. He lowered his voice back down to normal volume, wanting to appear calm and reasoned.

"Plus, think of Albert. Albert died of a broken heart, waiting for a bollocking allotment." Keith scanned the eyes of everyone assembled, trying to hold each person's gaze for a second or two. "Metcalfe as good as killed Albert."

He felt anger start to simmer, small at first but each neighbour seemed to set off the next until the whole crowd, even Val, were nodding agreement.

Eric raised his feeble voice. "I'm a poor pensioner. I want my money back!"

"I want my money back!" Shouted a female voice, not Val.

"Me too!"

"Yeah!"

"Ok, ok. Everyone!" Keith tried to focus. "Yes, we all want our money back. Good point. The question is: how do we get it?"

"Well." said Geoff. "Why don't we just ask him?"

"So I take it we can accept the minutes of our last meeting as approved?" Bryan eyed the committee members around the table and saw each of them give the slightest nod. There was a strange atmosphere in the draughty, scuffed magnolia hall this evening. It wasn't unusual for only a handful of non-committee members to turn up but for *none* to attend, that was different. The hall seemed more echoey than usual and, thought Bryan with surprise, he was even missing the intrusive interjections of Keith. Never mind, there was still time. They were only just getting started.

Or maybe the odd atmosphere was all in his head? After the man in the cowboy hat had stormed out of his house, Bryan had expected a knock on the door from the police. But nothing. He had put his old escape plan into readiness, in case. He always had his passport on him, some cash to hand, and a carry-on bag permanently packed under the stairs. It had always been his intention that, should anything go wrong, he would catch a flight to Jamaica and see out his days in a sunny clime where rheumatism would be alleviated by warmth and the ready availability of marijuana.

But there had been no knock. Bryan had put his bag in

the boot of his car but maybe it wasn't going to be needed at all. The man had gone all weird when the name McKenna had been mentioned and his parting words seemed to suggest that he no longer had an interest in Bryan. Bigger fish to fry. Maybe, we'll see. Meanwhile, Bryan had a meeting to chair.

"Ok. Item #1 on the agenda. Financial statement for the quarter. Andy?"

Andy stood up and started handing out two stapled sheets around the table. While the sound of paper shuffling rose and fell there was a sudden clatter of a firedoor being thrown open and the unmistakeable sound of many people barging through the entryway. The door to the village hall burst open and a dozen or more people stormed in, a puce-looking Keith at their head.

"Gie us back our money, you thieving bastard!"

"Excuse me, Mr Knox!" Bryan rose to his feet in indignation and held his right hand up to try and pause the crowd. What new madness was this? Barely had he restored his equilibrium after his encounter with an enraged cowboy and now this - a lynch mob with a very nasty look about them, it seemed, even if he recognised many as allotment owners. "Whilst I welcome WAG members to attend committee meetings, and I always have and will, I will ask that attendees respect due process and conduct themselves appropriately. Otherwise, they will be ejected."

"Eject yersel' you bastard! Gie us our money back!"

"What money?" Bryan looked at the angry, animated faces in the crowd and, confused, turned to Andy who still stood ready with his figures for Agenda Item #1. "Do you know what money Mr Knox is referring to, Andy?"

"It's nowt to do wi' Andy. You're the thief! You're the

one who needs to pay us back. Not your feckin' committee - you!"

"I beg your pardon?" Bryan retorted. "Explain yourself, Knox, or you will be asked to leave."

"No! You explain! Explain why you've tapped into eleven different electricity supplies, costing us all hundreds of pounds." Keith waved a tattered piece of paper in the air. "And then you can explain how you're going to pay each and every one of us back!"

Bryan saw the sheet of paper, let Keith's words register and - for a fleeting moment - time seemed to stand still. The air was sucked from the room and all sound went dead as Bryan felt his soul leave his body and rush from the hall, fleeing into the night. From somewhere up in the rafters he looked down on himself: a pale, portly, cardiganed gentleman trying his best under difficult circumstance, now faced with some mob vengeance and the realisation that here, at last, lay his ruin. A spasm of rheumatism shot through him, making his knees shake and throwing him back into himself.

There was a shout and the clatter of double-doors again when a woman burst into the hall.

"Fire! There's a fire at the allotments! Someone call the fire brigade!"

Immediately the fierce mood switched into one of general confusion, disorganised milling about and loud chatter, followed by everybody running out of the hall and into the night. Within seconds Bryan was alone, standing in silence as the doors swung emptily to and fro.

Stunned by this turn of events, he stood motionless for a while. How had these people discovered his meter taps? Why had their bills shot up? He didn't understand. But it suddenly dawned on him that, whatever mistake he'd made, the end result was that rather than stealing money from those redundancy bastards at Scottish Power he'd actually been increasing their revenues.

Bryan closed his eyes and bowed his head in defeat. As calmly and as tidily as he could, he scooped up all the meeting paperwork and headed home to his car.

When Keith reached the allotments, shed #19 was burning merrily. The rest of the crowd stood around watching, crying and oohing at the flames and sparks like it was a Bonfire Night display. Then something inside the shed ignited and there was a loud explosion. People flinched away and crouched down as a snowfall of plastic shrapnel and fluttering marijuana leaves descended all around them.

Here was their evidence, he thought. Any doubt now as to what Metcalfe had been up to must surely evaporate.

Keith wasn't a religious man - he'd heard of Epiphany but never had one. For him, Epiphany might just as well be the name of a pornstar. But now he looked at the scene and the swirling herbal confetti, the crowd stunned and quiet, the paper with the list of names in his hand seemed to rise up unbidden to his eyes, the writing swimming into focus. Suddenly it was all too clear what he had to do. He grabbed the shoulder of Geoff, the nearest person to him.

"Have you got a light?"

Geoff handed him a lighter and Keith raised it into the air, looked up to the stars and at the top of his voice shouted: "For Albert!"

By the time the fire brigade arrived every single one of the cannabis sheds was ablaze, the crowd were chanting "Albert, Albert." and the overpowering smell of burning weed filled the evening air.

SIX

It was his foot that kept him awake but it was the smell which made him get out of bed and hobble to the open window. Peeking through the curtains Paul saw the allotments ablaze, pockets of flames interspersed with muddy hoses and trampled vegetation. It looked like the Western front after the tanks had rolled through. The whole scene was awash in the scattering blue lights from two fire engines and an assisting police car. Paul well knew that one of those fires was shed #19 and that his hiding place - and his secret stash - was no more.

"What's up lumpa?" Shirley's sleepy voice came over his left shoulder.

"Fires at the allotments." Paul said, sadly.

"Really? Wow." But she didn't get up. "You okay?"

Paul stood and thought, his back still to Shirley. His foot twinged as if telling him to make his mind up, and he winced. Down below he could see a policeman talking to an agitated and dishevelled Keith and then speaking into the radio clipped to his lapel.

"Why are you standing on one leg?" Shirley asked.

Sighing, Paul turned to face her but couldn't bring himself to look her in the eye. "My foot hurts."

"Oh. Did you bang it?"

"No. It's... a condition."

"Well you should go to the doctors if it's bothering you."

"I have. They gave me something."

"Oh. Ok. Well take it then." She paused. "Why didn't you tell me? That you'd been to the doctors?"

Paul hung his head. "It's embarrassing."

"Going to the doctors? Ha! Men."

"No. That's not what's embarrassing." He took a deep breath. "I have gout."

"Really?"

"Yeah." There it was, the truth was out. He didn't feel better, like they say you will, he just felt defeated.

"What did they give you - Colchicine?"

"No. It was... what?" Paul met Shirley's eyes for the first time. "How do you know about that?"

"Oh, my Dad used to get gout. Suffered a lot from it in his later years. I got to learn all about it." She gave a kind smile. "Come back to bed. It must be painful."

"It is." Paul hobbled back towards the bed, shame-faced but now curious. "So... you don't mind?"

"Mind! What's there to mind about? You can't do much about it, can you really?"

"Well, people think you get gout because you drink too much." His mouth was a thin line. "I drink too much."

"Well, yes, lumpa - you do." Shirley smiled at him, kindly.

"Well you go to the pub every night!" Paul retorted.

"Yes, but only to look for you!" She snapped, then immediately regretted it. "Look, lover. Yes you can do things which alleviate gout, or reduce the incidence of it - lifestyle changes, dietary changes and so on. But a large part of it is simply hereditary. There's only so much you can do about it. And, it's good to share."

"Really?" Paul brightened.

"Yes, really! What did the doctor say?"

"Dunno. Didn't want to hang around." Paul hung his head again. "Just wanted medicine and to get the hell out."

"Oh, lumpa! Come here." Shirley reached across the bed to give him a hug and he leant into it. "Take your medicine then and try and get some sleep."

"I can't."

"Well... try."

"No, I mean I can't take my medicine."

"Why not?"

Paul paused, then muttered into her hair. "I lost it."

"You lost it?" Shirley cocked her head, unsure.

"Yeah. I had it in this little tin see-"

Shirley's eyes widened and she sat upright, pulling out of the hug. "That was your pills?"

Paul was taken aback by her reaction. "Aye."

"I thought it was..." She blurted and then stopped herself.

"What? What did you think it was?"

"Nothing."

Paul searched her face and lowered his voice. "Shirl. I've shared with you. I was embarrassed about my gout but I shared it with you. So, tell me... what did you think was in it?"

Shirley looked into her lover's puppy-dog eyes and sighed. "A ring. I thought you were going to propose."

"Propose!" Paul blurted and then immediately regretted it.

"What? Is it so unlikely?"

"Er... no."

"Oh, great. Marvellous." Shirley crossed her arms, her face set.

"Shirl!" Paul implored but Shirley huffed, pulled the duvet up over her shoulder and tucked herself in facing the wall, her back to him. "Shirl!"

"Never mind, *Shirl.*" Shirley said, tight-lipped. "Tomorrow you're going on a diet."

"It's good to share, right?." Paul asked.

"Not in my experience." Cullen said, looking out over Elibank woods.

"Yeah. No. Shirl says... but... well..." He exhaled long and hard. "Kinda buggered now to be honest."

"How come?"

"Well first off, I'm currently about as popular with Shirl as someone caught throwing poo at Dame Judi Dench."

"Who?"

"Second, she wants to put me on a bloody diet now. Got to cut down on meat and drink. Meat and drink? Clues in the bloody name!"

"Why?"

"Erm... weight?" Paul wasn't ready to share the fact he had gout with Cullen just yet. He patted his stomach to reinforce his alibi.

Cullen tried to smirk. "Exercise. That's the key."

"I get plenty of exercise!" Paul complained. "It's called work. You should try it."

Cullen didn't spot the little dig. "What would you rather do? A) - go on a vegetarian diet; or B)-"

"B!"

"I didn't say what B was."

"Doesn't matter." Paul was glum. "Maybe I should get away for a bit. Go somewhere new."

"Try the moon. You'll weigh less there."

"Ha bloody Ha. You're all heart."

"It could be worse."

"It is worse! I didn't get around to point number three."

"Which is?"

"Which is: now I can't even propose to her. Which, you may remember, had been my plan."

"Course you can."

"No. I. Can't." Paul glared at Cullen as if explaining to a simpleton. "Because now she'll think I'm only proposing because she mentioned it first. She'll think it was her idea. She's forced me into it!"

"Oh come on. Does it matter?"

"Yes!" Paul waggled his eyes, dementedly. "I'm going to have to wait ages now, so I can make it look like a genuine proposal."

"I think you're over-thinking this."

"Oh do you?" Paul snarked. "And how many times have you proposed?"

Cullen froze. "Once." He said quietly.

"Sorry, mate. Didn't think." Paul bit his lip and they both sat saying nothing for a long time. Unexpectedly it was Cullen who broke it.

"I need to go away for a while."

Paul tried to lighten the mood. "How will I tell?"

"I'll let you know when I'm back."

"Where you gonna go?"

"Away."

"Why?"

"I need to get something out of my system."

"Is that all I'm going to get?" Paul sighed, but something about Cullen's demeanour made him wait. Eventually Cullen said: "McKenna."

"McKenna? McKenna? McKenna? Rings a ... Tyler the teenage tealeaf?"

Cullen nodded. "His father."

"Huh. What about him?"

"Shed #19 used to be his."

"Wow! OK. So?"

By way of no answer at all, Cullen stood up and zipped up his tired waterproof.

"It's good to share, remember?" Paul prodded, hopefully.

Cullen looked down at his friend with weary eyes. "One day."

POSTSCRIPT

Bryan Metcalfe was arrested at Edinburgh airport as he boarded the Virgin Atlantic flight to JFK. He was tried at Selkirk Sheriff Court and convicted on eleven counts of criminal damage, theft of electricity under Section 13 of the Theft Act and production of a controlled drug as defined by the Misuse of Drugs Act 1971. The Sheriff, taking Bryan's age and public service record into account, gave him the maximum fine of £2000, ordered him to pay reparation of £850 to each of the affected residents and sentenced him to nine month's Community Service repairing a number of allotments in Walkerburn. Bryan's summary dismissal from his post on the Walkerburn Community Council prompted a front-page article in the Peeblesshire News under the headline *Councillor fired for not keeping off the grass.*

Keith Knox was unanimously elected Chairman of the Walkerburn Allotment Group and held their first meeting around a brazier at the allotments where they all ceremonially burnt Bryan's paperwork. He agreed to fix Paul's van free of charge after Paul ran a new tap for him on the other side of the meter. He is going to the Pub Quiz at the Lamb & Flag for the first time next month.

Shirley Stevenson has started both Paul and herself on a new healthy dietary and fitness regime and severely restricted his intake of processed meat and alcohol. She keeps a regular check on his gout and has decided that, if he can keep it at bay for a period of three months, she will introduce Paul to her mother. She hasn't told Paul this.

"Big" Paul McInnes has fixed the leak in his cabin roof and now divides his time between there and Shirley's. When he got his van back from Keith the first thing he did was check for the small plush box he kept hidden in his glove compartment. It was still there. Three times a week he now eats a full English breakfast at the Scots Pine diner on the A703. He hasn't told Shirley this.

Mungo James Cullen has not been seen for a while.

AUTHOR'S NOTE

This book is not intended to condone or encourage cannabis use, or any other drugs. Even if, at least in Scotland, cannabis seems to be a, ahem, growth industry. I'm a boring bloke with no history of drug use ever - shocking I know - so research was required to write this story and I found account after account of police discovering illicit cannabis farms in homes, outbuildings and, yes, at least one shed.

I'd also like to point out that tampering with electricity meters and supplies is not only illegal but dangerous. Big Paul tells me he has never done it, and nor should you. Neither has he ever had gout, so please don't write in to tell me that it can be very painful and debilitating. I know. Paul's condition here is deliberately mild. He's on medication to alleviate it but will also be subject to some lifestyle changes in future books, if Shirley has her way!

As for Walkerburn, it is a small village by the Tweed, quite unremarkable, although there are some cracking walks in the area. No wonder Cullen likes it. It does have some allotments but no WAG - and those allotments, as perhaps befits a small village, are half the size of those I describe here. It also has a Community Council which is probably nothing like the one I depict and probably would not consider someone like Bryan a suitable candidate for membership. I chose Walkerburn as a setting because that's where Shirley's flat is, no other reason.

Thank you to Beta readers Deidre M, Pete B, Mike M and John K for their hugely valuable feedback and comments. They are extremely important to me and I am convinced this book is the better for them.

My biggest thanks go to my partner, Claire, who is always willing to listen to my ideas, offer suggestions and spot things which are a little off. And then tell me about them. At length. Until I change them.
Which is good. Honest.

Finally, this book marks the start of Cullen's backstory moving more centre stage. Up to now I have hinted at something here, dropped a cryptic reference there. It probably hasn't meant much but it all does make sense - trust me - and you will see this backstory knit together and become more prominent in future books in this series (yeah, it's a series! Didn't I tell you?). On the one hand I hope it makes the books richer and, well, moreish; on the other, it will mean they'll need to be read in order for things to make most sense. Sorry about that.

If you think that's a pain, you should try writing them. It's a bugger.

mjf
14.3.2020

Cullen and Big Paul will return in a full-length novel *Lay Misty For Me.*

If you enjoyed their adventures, why not join their fan club? You'll get early notice of this new book, special offers, a monthly newsletter from the author, unique free content, invitations for discounts and more!

JOIN at **download.markfarrer.com/signup**

Tell others what you thought...

If you enjoyed this book, please leave a review on Amazon

About the Author

You can learn more about Mark Farrer at **www.markfarrer.com** or follow him on Twitter **@mark_farrer.**

Printed in Great Britain
by Amazon

32823424R00066